Michael S. Weiner Esq grew up in New York State and graduated from the University of Albany. After college, he graduated from Touro Law School and became an admitted attorney in the state of New York. After practicing corporate and criminal law for several years, Weiner decided to become a middle school teacher for the New York Board of Education. Weiner still enjoys teaching, and is currently working on his next novel.

THE SCAR

The Scar has lived through many changes. I'd like to thank my family and friends who helped make it what it is today.

I also want to give a special thanks to Christine McDonough and Michele Nelson, for sharpening my writing, and vastly improving the manuscript.

Michael S. Weiner

THE SCAR

Vanguard Press

VANGUARD PAPERBACK

© Copyright 2010
Michael S. Weiner

A CIP catalogue record for this title is
available from the British Library.

ISBN 978 184386 657 2

*Vanguard Press is an imprint of
Pegasus Elliot MacKenzie Publishers Ltd.*
www.pegasuspublishers.com

First Published in 2010

**Vanguard Press
Sheraton House Castle Park
Cambridge England**

Printed & Bound in Great Britain

I dedicate this book to my loving parents. Without their wisdom, guidance and encouragement, I would not have strived to reach my dreams.

This book is also dedicated to my lovely wife, Diana. Thank you for believing in me, and inspiring me to follow my dream of writing. You never let me give up on myself, and you motivate me to be better than I am.

Chapter 1

The Stranger

A little after ten P.M., there was a man standing in the shadows underneath a flickering lamppost located across the street from St. Paul's Church. The mysterious man kept his eyes steady on the front entrance waiting for Father Thomas Michael to make his exit. It is Father Michael's job to make sure the church is vacant and locked, secured from any late night intruders; making the reverend always the last person to leave.

Father Michael has been the high priest of St. Paul's Church for almost thirty years. He has hosted numerous charitable events that have earned him a great reputation of a warm, caring, compassionate man. For years, Sunday mass has been flooded with people to hear his powerful, uplifting sermons. Newspapers and television news stations frequently run stories, praising the kind priest for his teachings, sound advice, and his loyalty to the community.

Twenty-five minutes past ten, a congregate of people exited the church and thirty minutes later, Father Michael finally made his exit. Just moments before the priest turned the key to lock the church and go home, the man standing in the darkness ran from the shadows, only to trouble the priest for one last confession inside the church. It is a canon for a priest to listen to a spontaneous request to hear a confession if only the request is reasonable. Since the request came only minutes after closing, the kind priest agreed to hear what the stranger had to say.

After Father Michael and the unknown man entered the church, the priest locked the door from the inside so no others could enter. "I would like to get home at a reasonable hour tonight," the elderly, kind priest said, as his reason for locking the door. Inside the church, candles illuminated just enough light for the priest and the stranger to find their way around.

The priest escorted the stranger to the confessional located in the middle of the church. The confessional was made of wood and it portrayed many celestial references to the son of God, and God Himself. Behind the confessional doors was a room separated by a thin panel with a fixed grille no higher than five feet from the bottom. The priest extended his hand and pointed to the door in which he wanted the stranger to enter. As the stranger entered the confessional, Father Michael entered through a separate door on the adjacent side.

Inside the poorly lit confessional, both the stranger and the priest sat in the comfort of cushioned seats and in an atmosphere of privacy. With a desire to get home as fast as he could, Father Michael immediately asked how he could help the stranger.

"Bless me, Father, for I have sinned. It has been over a year since my last confession." The priest sat silently. "Father, I am holding something inside me that is burning a hole through my heart. It is worse than any mere impure thought and more sinful than any act one could ever imagine. It is nothing but the purest of immorality. And I know this because I feel the wickedness flowing through my every vein." The stranger paused for a short while not knowing if he wanted to continue.

"My son, if you want forgiveness you must tell me what it is you are holding inside," the priest declared.

"Father, I don't understand what good will come from revealing what I have come to believe is unforgivable."

"Then why is it you came tonight other than to confess your sins?" Father Michael said with a short pause. "My son, I cannot hold your hand if you will not reach it out to me."

"I wonder sometimes if there really is a God, and if He would ever forgive me for what I have done," the stranger muttered.

"God can see the true nature in every action and only He can judge you."

"Ha," the stranger sighed. "You say that as if you really know."

"Son, we will all believe what we want to believe. I have chosen to believe in the words I preach and try to help others with the words I believe in. Certainty is one luxury we do not have, so we must do what we think is right and pray that the choices we make are the right ones."

"Father, can I trust you?"

"Son, I am a man of the cloth. My trust is unconditional."

"Then it troubles me greatly Father," the stranger whispered and then once again paused in silence.

"You must tell me what it is that troubles you or I cannot be of any help to you."

"It is not the fact that I have killed in cold blood. It's the pain Father, the pain portrayed in the faces I watch suffer while they beg for help. The screaming inside my head I can see, but I cannot hear and the slow drops of fallen tears from the eyes of every helpless victim. But you know what troubles me the most Father?" the stranger questioned.

The priest had heard many confessions throughout his work as a priest; a slip of a dirty word, a cheating spouse, an act of omission, but never a confession that made him scared for his own safety. Not knowing if he should continue with this confession or run for the door, Father Michael replied, "I do not know what troubles you the most, my son."

"What troubles me the most Father, is that you would offer me forgiveness."

Before the father could even reply, he heard the stranger storm out of the confessional and stop no further than the door in front of him. Not knowing what was about to occur, the priest's heart began to race with fear. Droplets of sweat instantly rained from his open pores, as his nerves rattled his inner bones. The confessional door slowly began to open, penetrating a small amount of light through the aperture of the door.

In a second's time, the priest was trapped, surrounded by wooden planks, old age, and a firearm pointed at his head. Although the reverend couldn't fathom why the stranger wanted to place a gun in his face, the priest didn't bother asking him for a reason. Instead, Reverend Michael declared firmly, "God will never forgive you for this," hoping to strike fear in the stranger.

"It's okay Father, God will not have to," the stranger said, as he rammed the tip of his gun into the priest's mouth, breaking five of his front teeth. At first, Father Michael put up a little fight, but the stranger overpowered him with his strength, eventually causing the priest to tire quickly.

In the back of Father Michael's mind, he mumbled a prayer for God to help him from the deadly fate that lay ahead of him. But there was no bolt of lightning from the sky, and there was no twist of fate, there was only the sound of a nine millimetre semi-automatic weapon that claimed the life of the dear old Father Michael.

Chapter 2

The very next morning, Detective David Seff received a telephone call from his partner, Mitchell Jacobs. The call was to report to St. Paul's Church as quickly as possible. "There was a high profile murder last night and the captain wants us leading the case. It seems someone shot the famous Father Thomas Michael. What is this world coming to?" The detective wasted no time and rushed out the door of his apartment, driving toward St. Paul's Church.

Detective Seff lived in Pittsburgh, Pennsylvania, thirty-five minutes away from where Father Michael was brutally murdered. On the way to the crime scene, the detective took out a recently purchased pack of cigarettes from his glove compartment. There were only two sticks of tobacco remaining in the pack. Detective Seff has been working on the police force for a little over twelve years. His addiction to cigarettes began around the same time.

David Seff was promoted to detective just after two years of walking the beat. He was a tough cop who did not take lip from anyone other than his superiors. During the first three years as a detective, he was only assigned to investigate petty crimes in which no one really cared if they were solved or not. However, Seff tried to get to the bottom of every case placed on his desk, no matter how insignificant the assignment was. His diligence and hard work did not go unnoticed, and the captain of the squad began to delegate more imperative cases for him to solve. By his fourth year as a detective, Seff was working strictly homicide cases, and by his ninth year, he managed to solve more murders than any other detective in his department.

When the detective arrived at the church, he had no choice but to park a block away because of the amount of press swarming around the police barricade looking for the facts. As

Seff walked through the crowd, he ignored the journalists and made his way to the front of the church. His partner, Detective Jacobs, was waiting for him at the front entrance. "So, what do we have here?" Detective Seff inquired, wasting no time.

"One very unlucky dead priest," Mitchell replied, as they entered the church and made their way to the dead body. "He was found around seven this morning by Father Schmitt."

"Has Father Schmitt already been questioned?"

"Only by the primary officers that were first to the scene. They're holding him in the back corner of the church for when we're ready to talk to him."

"What were they able to find out?"

"Not a whole lot. When he came in this morning, the front door of the church was unlocked, and the first thing he saw was Father Michael with two holes in his head and he immediately called the police. The detectives made their way to the dead body and Detective Seff quickly examined the late Father Michael. "The dead body was found as you see it; in a sitting position, next to the confessional. The forensic specialist noticed that the hinge on the confessional door was forcefully ripped from the frame, which probably means there was some kind of struggle between the priest and the killer, or killers."

"The bastard shot both of his eyes right through the back of his head," Detective Seff said, staring at Father Michael's wounded face.

"And one time in his chest as well."

"Did forensics find anything else?"

"It's actually what they didn't find. All three bullets used to kill the priest and their casings are missing. The killer dislodged the bullets out from a bench two rows behind where the body was discovered. If you look, you can see the indentations in the bench where the bullets were extracted. The crime scene specialists determined that the three holes in the bench were most likely made by bullets from a nine millimetre handgun."

"Did the killer take the priest's wallet?" Detective Seff asked.

"No, it was found in his back pocket with sixty-three dollars and all his credit cards."

"Well, I guess we can rule out robbery as a motive," Detective Seff deducted.

"Don't look now, but the captain is here and he doesn't look very happy."

Following the same path as Detectives Seff and Jacobs, Captain William Baron walked directly over to the detectives. Captain Baron was a quick talker and a man who gets right to the point.

"Good morning, Captain," both detectives said one after the other.

"You call this a good morning, a dead priest in our backyard? I got a shit storm of reporters outside. You better believe this is making the front pages of every paper in the city. The mayor called the chief and told him that he wants me to do a press conference. At my age, I don't need this kind of stress. Here's the deal, I'm going to announce that you're going to be leading the investigation into Father Michael's death, and I will be overseeing your every action," Captain Baron said, staring at Detective Seff. "This case is your top priority and the only thing you're working on until it gets solved."

"Yes sir, Captain," Seff replied.

"Look over the body, interview whoever you have to interview, and then I want you to look up the address of a man named Irving Adelson. He and I were in the academy together. I believe he retired about four years ago. I want you to visit this man; there might be a chance that he could help you with this case."

"Not for nothing, but how is your friend going to help us solve this case?" Detective Seff asked.

"When you see him and he's willing to help, tell him exactly how you found the body, and don't leave out any details." Right after the captain retorted, he walked away, turning his back to the detectives and ultimately leaving the church to make his speech to the press.

+ depredador

Chapter 3

The Mind of the Stranger

I am a man who has no face, but I carry many names. I have been called a vicious stalker, a thief, and a dangerous murderer that preys on his victims. I have also been called a hero. Which name actually defines me is something I will never know until it is my day of judgment. I do not take pride in what I do, but I do take full responsibility for it. That is the risk I have chosen to take.

I have not attended church in over thirty years, but I owed a confession that was long overdue. I have always believed in a higher power, however, I never followed one particular faith. I have trouble believing in what I cannot see, and I can only follow what I know. There are many people in this world searching for the truth I possess. Some would say I have been blessed by the angels from heaven, although it can just as easily be said I have been sanctified by the devil himself. I have contemplated this enigma in my mind for many years. And I have come to believe I am both, structured by the hands of heaven and shaped by the mind of hell, a creation of a means to an end.

My umbilical chord choked me to death before my body ever felt life. The doctors had to perform a cesarean section on my mother to save me. By the time I was out of my mother's uterus, I had stopped breathing for more than two minutes. While the doctors were doing their best to bring me back to life, my mother went into hypovolemic shock. The doctors could not save her and she passed away from uncontrollable internal bleeding. My father never forgave me.

I cannot tell you what happened during the time I was dead, but the moment I started to breathe, I was different. I was given a power that some might call a gift. I was able to

see the past of human wickedness that lingers around the mortal soul. It is portrayed in colours and each colour means something different. Father Michael emitted nothing but the purest of evil and I therefore had no choice but to end his life.

I sometimes think about what my life would be like if my mother didn't die. How many things in my life would be different? There would be a chance my family would be whole, and I might have grown up without the thirst for blood. That is a dream I have come to desire, but know will never come true.

I also desire more than impossible dreams. I desire a life I can call my own, but that day may never come. I have a job I must do for which I have come to believe brought me back from death: to punish those who are undeserving of life.

forward - adelante
CRAPPY - de mierda, asqueroso

Chapter 4

After Detectives Seff and Jacobs finished examining the body
of Father Michael and questioning Father Schmitt, they did as
Captain Baron instructed. Irving Adelson lived on the
opposite side of town forty minutes away. He lived in an
apartment complex two blocks away from the projects, an
awful place for a person to retire.

"Is this what we have to look forward to when we retire,
a crappy pension and a penthouse view of the ghetto?"
Detective Jacobs said just seconds before he knocked on
Irving's apartment door.   un poco

Mr. Adelson's door opened slightly, hindered by a chain
lock attached to the door. A man with a middle-aged face
poked his head through the opening and said, "Can I help you
gentlemen?"

"Are you Irving Adelson?" Detective Seff asked.

"Yes, that's me."

"This is Detective Jacobs and I'm Detective Seff. We
were sent by Captain William Baron. He told us that you
might have information about a homicide case we're
currently investigating."   homicide

"I'm going to need to see some ID and badges." insignias

Detective Seff and Jacobs reached into their jacket
pockets, took out their badges, and held them up for Mr.
Adelson to view. Afterward, Irving unlocked the chain from
the door and both detectives entered the apartment. "You
could never be too careful these days. Please come in and
make yourself at home." Mr. Adelson's apartment was built
for one person. It consisted only of a tiny living room, one
bedroom, and a small walk-in kitchen. Mr. Adelson kept little
chocolate candy wrapped in gold foil in a bowl by the front
door. To show his hospitality, he grabbed a handful of
candies and pleasantly forced it into the hands of the

agarro

detectives. "These chocolates are so good, you have to try some. Before I sit down to talk with you, can I get you something to drink, water, cola, coffee?"

"No, thank you sir, but maybe you can help us some other way," Detective Seff said, as he and Detective Jacobs sat on Mr. Adelson's living room couch.

"Well then, how can I help you?"

"I'm not exactly sure. Our captain seems to think you might have certain knowledge about a murder that happened last night over at St. Paul's Church."

"Well, I don't know anything about a murder. I haven't been to St. Paul's Church since I was a little kid, nor would I care to. You see, I'm not really a religious man. So who was it that died?"

"Father Thomas Michael," Detective Jacobs responded.

"Now why does that name sound familiar?" Irving replied.

"Maybe you've seen him on television. He's known to be in the public eye every now and again."

"Maybe, but I don't see how I can help. I really don't even know who he is."

"Our captain told us to inform you of every detail surrounding the death. Maybe the way Father Michael died might sound familiar. He was shot once in each eye and in his chest by his heart," Detective Seff said.

"Did the killer leave a marking on his back, some type of symbol carved into his body?" Irving quickly questioned.

"We never checked. The priest was fully clothed at the crime scene," Detective Jacobs responded.

"What makes you think our victim has a symbol carved in his back?" Detective Seff asked.

"You can call it a hunch, but your killer's MO sounds somewhat familiar."

Detective Seff whispered into his partner's ear and told him to call the medical lab. "Father Michael's body should have arrived there by now. See if someone there can quickly

23

examine Father Michael for some type of marking carved in his body."

"Excuse me for a moment," Detective Jacobs said, as he stepped into the corner of the room and quietly made the call.

"You said the killer's MO sounded familiar, how so?" Detective Seff asked.

"It sounds just like a case I was once assigned to, probably before you were popping pimples and chasing girls around the playground."

Detective Jacobs sat back down next to Detective Seff and whispered into his ear, "The body is being processed right now in the medical lab. One of the lab technicians is going to call back in a few minutes and let us know if there are any markings."

Detective Seff brought his attention back to Mr. Adelson. "Tell us more about this case you were working on."

"Well, about thirty years ago, I was assigned to a homicide case. I was a young detective at the time. It was one of my first homicide cases. When my partner, Darryl Rivers, and I arrived at the crime scene, we found the victim pretty much identical to the way you just described yours, except there was a marking on the victim's lower back. A marking we could never figure out. It was the most gruesome thing I've ever seen.

"The killer didn't leave any clues for us to find. No fingerprints, no weapon, and no trail to follow. My partner and I had no leads and nothing to go on. The only thing we could do is wait around for the killer to strike again. Four days later, another body was found the same way as our first victim. Our killer happened to be very good at keeping his identity and whereabouts a secret. The popular opinion was that the killings were done at random, so the only thing we really had to go on was the markings carved in the bodies.

"We tried to match the symbol to different cultural alphabets, gang signs, Egyptian hieroglyphics, anything we could think of, but nothing matched up, so we had no other

random al azar

choice but to wait for the killer to strike again. A week went by before the killer murdered again. This time the victim was a thirteen-year-old boy in a park, playing by himself. This was the first killing done during daylight hours. It just so happens that a witness saw another teenager run out of the park and into a house two blocks away, just moments after he heard the sound of three gunshots.

"My partner and I didn't waste any time. We took five officers and ran over to the house the teenager was seen running into. We knew we were dealing with a person who wasn't afraid to kill, so we didn't bother announcing our presence. Instead, my partner kicked the front door open, and I led the officers inside.

"The teenager was taking a shower at the time, so none of us were in any real danger. My partner found a nine millimetre gun stashed inside a box on the top shelf of the teenager's closet along with a very sharp knife. We arrested the boy and took him down to the station. The teenager's name was Jake Weans. Wound up the boy was eighteen years old, never graduated from high school because of severe mental and behavioral problems, and had bounced around from group homes to foster care families since he was thirteen. The kid was crazy, didn't have a stable mind. When my partner and I sat down to take his statement, all he would do is repeat the same thing over and over again. 'I can see evil. The only people I have killed were bad men.' → desalojar

"We discovered that the bullets that were dislodged from the victims' bodies came from Jake Weans' gun. The knife we found also had traces of all three of the victims' blood. It was a slam dunk case for the prosecution. We had a witness who placed Jake at the scene of the third murder, and we had the murder weapon with Jake's fingerprints on it. There wasn't a jury that could possibly find Jake Weans innocent.

"However, Jake Weans' attorney made a motion to the court to have the gun and knife suppressed along with any other evidence found directly or indirectly, due to an illegal search and seizure. Jake's attorney argued that my partner

bullets → labalos.

and I entered Mr. Weans' place of residency without a proper search warrant, violating his fourth amendment constitutional right.

"Because the witness in the park didn't see the kid carrying a weapon, the judge decided that entering his house without a search warrant was a violation of his constitutional rights. Therefore, the gun, confession, knife, and the blood found on the knife were suppressed, and the district attorney didn't have enough evidence to prosecute Jake Weans. He was walking the street again that very next day a free man.

"My partner and I were criticised in every newspaper around the area for our poor police work. Our pictures made some of the newspapers' front page. We embarrassed our captain and humiliated the department. As soon as the story broke, our captain immediately took us off the street and we wound up riding a desk for the rest of our careers. My partner and I became a joke around the department. That case destroyed my career as a detective, and rid me of any opportunity for a promotion.

"Looking back, that case could have put my career on the fast track of being a first-grade detective. Jake Weans should be serving a life sentence right now, but because of my mistake, as far as I know, he's somewhere still walking around a free man."

"Do you think Jake Weans could be the guy we're looking for now?" Detective Jacobs asked.

"Well, Jake would be in his late forties, and still very capable of committing a crime such as the one you described."

"It might be helpful to talk to your old partner about this case as well. Can you tell us where we can find him?" Detective Seff asked.

"I'm afraid that's impossible. Darryl died six years ago to liver cancer."

Abruptly, the sound of Detective Jacobs' cellular phone went off. "It's the medical lab, excuse me for a moment," Detective Jacobs said and walked into the adjacent room.

"Detective Seff, if it just so happens that the killer you're looking for is Jake Weans, make sure you capture him by the book, and make sure he never sees the light of day again. His victims deserve justice."

Detective Jacobs walked back into the room with a slight grin on his face. "The lab found a marking carved into Father Michael's lower back. We should go."

"Yeah, I guess we should. Well, thank you for your time, Mr. Adelson. We appreciate your help." Detective Jacobs and Seff walked quickly to the door.

"You fellows let me know how this case turns out."

"If we catch the killer, we'll let you know."

Chapter 5

History of the Stranger

I have killed many people in my lifetime, and the truth is I can't remember them all, but I can remember my first kill vividly. I was only thirteen at the time. My father became an alcoholic soon after my mother died. My maternal grandmother refused to let my sister and me stay with or see our father when he was drunk, so we hardly saw him at all. He would visit every now and again, but eventually the visits stopped. Eight years later, my grandmother died from old age, and we had no choice but to live with our father. My father's drinking habit never subsided; it only grew worse over the years. He worked for a shipping company where most of the employees were either high on something or intoxicated. But as long as they got the job done, no one cared.

When my sister and I first moved in with my father, he was very kind to us. He said it was nice to have a family again. However, his attitude quickly changed when all the responsibilities of parenting came knocking at the door. The responsibilities just inspired him to drink more, so he would become obliterated and forget my sister and I ever existed. My father made several attempts to sober up, but his attempts never lasted more than the thought itself.

My sister is four and a half years older than I am, so she took it upon herself to take care of me. She would make sure I ate, tutored me with my class work, and made sure I went to bed on time. The only thing my father did was lay on the couch with a beer in his hand. In time, he became invisible to me, but that was until I turned eleven and the beatings started. I didn't mind the beatings, just as long as my father didn't hit my sister. After a while, the beatings stop hurting and the pain was something I just learned to absorb. My father said he was

STICH - puntada, punzada.
beat - golpear, pegar
dar una paliza

doing me a favour because he was making me into a man, and to survive in this world, I had to be tough. FUERTE He wanted me to be grateful, so after each beating I told him how appreciative I was. In all honesty, I wasn't grateful or appreciative, but as long as he didn't lay a finger on my sister, I was content.

My sister was never around for the beatings, so she never knew, or at least I thought she didn't. I wanted to tell her, but I was afraid she would confront my dad and receive a beating herself. I remember when my father knocked my front tooth out with the back of his hand. My sister thought it was so cute that I lost a tooth; she put a five dollar bill underneath my pillow case and pretended it came from the tooth fairy. My father was a bastard, if only she knew.

From the first time my father beat me, I wished him dead, but as I turned thirteen, he was regrettably still alive and still teaching me how to be a man. During the years, I experienced bruised ribs, a broken arm, cigarette burns all over my backside, the taste of gasoline in my mouth, and twenty-six stitches without child services ever finding out. I was one TORPE clumsy child, but as long as my father didn't touch my sister, I didn't care.

My sister was eighteen and starting to look more and more like the photographs of my mother. Their facial features were identical. My father must have thought the same as I did, since he would sometimes mistakenly call her my mother's name. I remember one night I awoke from a scary dream, and I tried to fall back asleep, but my mouth was so dry I couldn't concentrate on anything else. Consequently, I went downstairs bend to the kitchen to get myself a glass of water. In the kitchen, I vuelta found my sister bent over a chair naked with my dad behind her with his pants down to his ankles. I'll never forget the tears SLIT on my sister's face. muñeca corta My sister slit her wrists and killed herself that very night. abrir And just like my mother, my father blamed me. All this time, I guess my sister knew the extent of how bad our father really was. I discovered my sister's dead body only moments before my father did. I knew as soon as he discovered my sister, he

RIB - costilla
REGRET - arrepenti _, remordi
REGRETTABLE - lamentable
BRUISE - contusionar, machacar, moretón

would come looking for me. My sister was gone, so I had no reason to take anymore of his beatings; that's when I decided it was time to take a stand. I stabbed my father over thirty-six times that night. He never knew what hit him.

My father expected that I would sit still while he tortured me, as I usually did. But as my father pulled his arm back and wound up to hit me, his chest became an open target and that's where I stabbed him first. As I was stabbing him repeatedly, I wasn't thinking about all the times he beat me and left me bleeding and bruised, I thought about my sister and how I will never see her smile again. With every thrust of my knife I screamed, but I didn't cry until I stopped.

After I killed my father, I didn't go into shock; instead, I stayed focused on what I had to do. For the moment, time was my enemy, and I had to start moving. I didn't have to pack my belongings because I've been planning to run away for some time now. The only reason why I stayed was for my sister, except she was dead now, and my reason for staying was gone.

I grabbed my backpack underneath my bed that was full of clothes, certain toiletries, some dry food, and a picture of my sister. I was going to need something else though, something essential for my escape: money. I went into my father's closet where he kept his secret stash of seventy-five dollars. I searched my sister's room for money, but I couldn't find any. I could have tried to grab my father's wallet out of his back pocket, but I didn't want to see his ugly face again.

I left the house on my dirt bike as fast as I could. I didn't know where I was headed, but I was trying to get as far away from my house as possible. As I was riding my bicycle, I thought about two things. The first was how far seventy-five dollars was going to take me. The second was a colour; the radiance that surrounded my father, it was dark and dreadful. The colour was mostly black, but it had a tint of orange. It was a colour I've seen outlining many other individuals, so I thought it would be best if I stayed away from people like that.

30

Chapter 6

Detective Seff and Jacobs drove to the medical lab. On the way there, Detective Seff called police headquarters to talk with Detective Terry Garder. Terry was Seff's first partner when he became a detective: "Hi, Terry, it's David. I'm going to need you to do a couple of things for me."

"Hold on, let me get a pad and find a pen," Detective Garder replied. Terry is a talented detective. She works very hard and is extremely committed to the job. As much as Detective Garder would like to, she doesn't walk the street anymore. Six years ago, Terry was shot from behind in the spinal chord and became paralysed from the waist down. Because of her injury, Terry is confined to a wheelchair, and behind a desk. Her desk is always a mess, but nonetheless, she is very organised. "Okay, Dave, tell me what you need."

"I'm looking for a file that goes back about thirty years. The case name is Jake Weans. It was a homicide case. The primary detectives were Irving Adelson and Darryl Rivers. Before you look for the file though, I need you to search our records for Jake Weans' address, phone number, and any other information you can find out about him."

"Is this the guy responsible for the murder of Father Michael?" Terry asked.

"To tell you the truth, I'm not sure, but it's the best lead we have right now. Listen, I'm going to the medical examiner's office right now to get a better look at the body, and to see if the examiner found anything new. The moment you have any information, I need you to call me on my cell phone right away."

"I'll start right now and get back to you as soon as possible."

"Thank you, and remember time is of the essence."

At the medical lab, Detective Seff and Jacobs were taken into the room where Father Michael's body was being examined. The corpse was being scanned and studied by the lead medical examiner, Dr. David Sachs. Dr. Sachs has been a doctor for twenty-seven years and became department manager of the medical lab five years ago. He specifically works on high profile cases such as the one Detective Seff is assigned to.

"Come in, come in, don't be shy, and do your best not to mind the stench of death," Dr. Sachs suggested.

"Dr. Sachs, how are you? It's been a long time," Seff said, as he and Jacobs walked over to the autopsy table.

Dr. Sachs recognised Detective Seff's face, but he was having a hard time remembering his name. "I know the face, but you'll have to forgive me, I can't seem to remember your name."

"Detective Seff, and it's quite all right. We've only met once before and that was a little over six years ago."

"Yes, the senator's son wasn't it?"

"That's correct," Seff answered.

"It's a shame how that kid died."

"Agreed," Seff replied. "This is my partner Detective Jacobs."

"It's very nice to meet you," Jacobs said, shaking Dr. Sachs' hand.

"Likewise. Though if I do recall, you did have a beautiful young female partner the last time I saw you. Would it be rude of me to ask what happened to her?" Dr. Sachs asked, looking over at Detective Seff.

"She was shot on the job."

"Oh, I'm sorry to hear that. I hope everything turned out all right."

"She's doing fine. Now if we could concentrate on the task at hand."

"Of course, but there really isn't too much to tell. The late Father Michael died of multiple gunshot wounds. However, the shooter probably killed the priest with the first shot. The bullet entered through the chest and pierced the right side of his heart, more than likely killing him instantly. I'm sorry to say there isn't anything attention-grabbing about Father Michael's death, except the fact that his eyes were launched through the back of his head."

"What about the marking carved in his body?" Detective Seff asked.

"I found the marking on his lower back." Dr. Sachs turned the corpse on its side to show the detectives. Seff and Jacobs both meticulously stared at the unusual marking trying to decipher what it could mean, however, not one of them had the slightest idea. "I tried to figure out what the marking might mean, but I had no such luck. By the depth of the incision, muscle and skin contracture around the small cuts, I'm positive the killer wasn't using a very large blade. And if I had to guess, the killer used a single-edged knife."

"Why is that, Doctor?" Jacobs asked.

"Well, if we were dealing with a double-edged blade, the end points of each incision made by the killer would look like a shark's tail. However, the incisions that were inflicted on Father Michael come to a sharp point, which is commonly caused by a single-edged blade."

"I see."

"After I cleaned the wound, I took pictures of the marking. The pictures should be developed shortly. If you're willing to stick around, I'll give you a few copies."

"Yeah, that would be great," Detective Seff replied. Just moments later, Seff's cell phone vibrated in his pocket, so he excused himself and walked over to the opposite corner of the examination room. "Detective Seff here."

"Hey, it's me, Terry."

"Were you able to find anything out?"

"Yes, I did," Terry answered proudly. "Your suspect Jake Weans no longer goes by that name. Get this; his new name is Kevin Mason. He had it changed when he turned nineteen years old. His place of residency is listed at 15

Maplewood Road, in Douglasville, which is owned by a woman named Diana Rodriguez."

Detective Seff took out a little pad and a pen from his inside suit pocket. He quickly wrote the address on the first blank page. "That's only about ten minutes away from the church where the murder took place."

"I know. He also works for the town as a sanitation worker over at the Douglasville Landfill."

"Is that it?"

"Well, he doesn't have a criminal record, not even a parking violation under either name. You sure this might be the guy?"

"I'm not sure of anything yet. Do me another favour. Call his employer; ask him if he came into work this morning and if he's still there. Do your best not to tell him you're a cop because then he most likely won't talk to you. Say you're his friend or something to that effect. Were you able to locate his file yet?"

"I haven't had any luck thus far, but I'm working on it."

"All right, let me know when you do. And Terry, good work."

"Thank you, bye."

After the phone call, Seff walked back over to where Dr. Sachs and Jacobs were standing. "Mitchell, we have to go. Terry found the location of our possible suspect. Doctor, if you can please fax those pictures to my office, I would really appreciate it," Seff said, as he handed Dr. Sachs his business card. "The fax number is on the bottom."

"Sure, no problem, as soon as I have them in my possession I'll have my secretary fax them over to you."

"Thank you, and if you discover anything else about the body, my phone number is on the card as well."

"Will do. Be safe."

Detective Seff and Jacobs left the medical examiner's office and made their way to the car. Hoping Kevin Mason was home, the detectives drove to 15 Maplewood Road to question his whereabouts last night.

Chapter 7

The Journey of the Stranger and the Scar ~creating~

After I left my father and sister soaking in their own blood, I decided to ride my bicycle to the bus terminal. I was too young to buy a ticket without an adult, so I paid a homeless man begging for change outside the terminal to purchase one for me. The man didn't ask any questions except, "Where to, young man?" I wasn't sure, so I chose the only listing I could see through the foggy, terminal window, New York City.

After the poor man bought my ticket and placed it in my hands, I walked over to the bus marked for New York and handed the ticket to the bus driver. The driver ripped my ticket in half and instructed me to find a seat on the bus. Within ten minutes, the bus was on its way to New York, and I was on my way out of Pennsylvania. I slept for most of the bus ride and awoke from the loudness that New York City emanates.

When I got off the bus and onto the city streets, I didn't know where to go or what to do. The city sure was big, and I felt a little out of place. There were many lights and many people with many things to say, but I ignored them all. I thought it would be better to keep to myself for the time being. The long trip made me a bit hungry, so I took out some food from my backpack to snack on. That very first night in the big city, I must have walked for miles. I saw so many beautiful things that I will never forget. Still to this day, I remember how tall the Empire State Building was, and how bright the lights are in Times Square. Yet the thing I remember the most and can never seem to forget is how I received the very noticeable three-inch scar on the left side of my forehead.

When I came to New York City, the weather was warm, and I was able to sleep outside on a bench in Central Park. I spent most of my days walking around the big city and most of my nights finding my way back to my bench. One night, I was trying to find my way back from a voyage to the Lower East Side of the city, but everywhere I turned was another unfamiliar street. The streets were mostly empty, so I couldn't ask anyone for directions, not that I would because I didn't feel very safe in the area.

The further I walked the more lost I got. The day turned into night and it was getting awfully late. I was afraid I was going to have to spend the night on one of these dark deserted streets. However, suddenly, out of nowhere, a dark-coloured van raced around the corner and stopped right in front of me. The van just stayed motionless for about twenty seconds. The windows in the van were tinted so I couldn't see inside. I thought to myself to walk over to the driver's side window and kindly ask the driver for directions, but I wasn't sure if that was the most intelligent idea. I began to sense that it might be better if I started walking in the opposite direction, so I did.

— As I turned my back to the van, I clearly heard the van door slide open and footsteps get louder and closer. I swiftly looked behind me and saw four large men in dark masks running over in my direction. I did my best to quickly run away, but the men were too fast or I was too slow. Two of the men lifted me off the ground while another covered my mouth with his hand to muffle my voice. The van pulled up close and the men threw me in the back of the van.

I tried my best to fight my way out, but the men were too powerful. They forced my arms behind my back and taped them together by my wrists. Then the men stuck a cloth that smelled like feet into my mouth and placed a piece of duct tape over it, so my voice would be stifled. After that, the men wrapped my legs together and covered my face with a dark bag so I couldn't see anything but darkness.

SWIFTLY rápido
STUCK
STIFLET —Sofocar, reprimir
WRAPPED—

I won't lie; I was scared out of my mind. The situation even made me wish I never left Pennsylvania. I couldn't help but tremble with extreme nervousness. We drove for a very long time. How long I can't say for certain, but in the uncomfortable position I was in, it felt like weeks, even though it was more like hours. When the van finally stopped, I heard everyone exit, yet they left me there by myself for a long time. While I was alone, I did my best to loosen the tape around my wrists, but I was unable to break free. And since there was no place for me to go to the bathroom, I had no choice but to make in my pants.

Eventually, someone came and opened the back door, dragged me out of the van, and lifted me over their shoulder, carrying me for quite a while. By the sound of the man's footsteps and the feel of gravity, I know I was carried up at least three flights of stairs. As the person carrying me came to a halt, I started to hear muffled voices in the background. I couldn't make out the words because they were speaking in a foreign language. Then I heard a door open and the voices became clearer, but I still couldn't understand what they were saying.

From out of the blue, my transport took me inside the room and forcefully threw me on a chair. There was an exchange of words between three different voices that sounded like arguments, but once again, I wasn't exactly sure. I tried my best to stop shaking, but my fear was so strong that I couldn't overcome it. Then all of a sudden, the bag covering my face was removed. The light in the room blinded me for a moment and I had to let my eyes adjust.

As soon as I was able to see clearly, I quickly looked around. Inside the room, there were five men; four that were extremely massive in height, muscle and weight, and one shorter smaller, thinner man. The short man was wearing an expensive pinstripe suit while the other four were wearing black jeans and jumpsuits. The man in the suit sat down behind a desk that was positioned in front of me and lit a cigar. The other men stood in the four corners of the room.

"My apologies for the way my men snatched you off the street and brought you here, but it's the way we do business," the man in the costly suit said who was apparently the person in charge. "If I had to read your mind, I bet you're wondering where you are, and what it is we're going to do with you. Well, while they're both exceptionally excellent questions, the real question you should be asking is how am I going to get out of here?" The man paused as if he wanted me to contemplate the question for a moment.

"There are two things we let boys your age do around here, and that's fight or prostitute. And when I say prostitute, I don't mean having the pleasure of servicing a beautiful woman. We don't have that type of clientele here. Instead, you're thrown in a room, sometimes tied up like the way you are now, sometimes chained to a bed. Then a disgusting, perverted man you do not know takes you in ways that will haunt you for the rest of your life. Sometimes they pay to give it to you, and sometimes they pay just to fondle you, either way, trust me, it's not a pleasant experience. Yet after you produce, roughly about forty thousand dollars for us, we drop you off in the middle of nowhere and we forget you exist.

"Now if you choose to fight, and you win seven fights in a row, we throw you back in the van, the same way you came, and drop you in the same place we found you." The man in charge paused once again and then ordered the muscle on my left to remove the tape covering my mouth. The muscle did as he was told and vigorously ripped the tape off my face with one hard tug. I immediately spit up the cloth that was forcefully placed in my mouth and coughed uncontrollably.

While I was repeatedly coughing, the man in the suit opened a mini-refrigerator located to the left of his desk, and pulled out a bottle of water. Then he walked around the desk to where I was situated, and as soon as my coughing came to a stop, he lifted my head back and gradually poured the water into my mouth. I was so dehydrated I easily swallowed the whole bottle.

"Now, kid, I'm going to give you a choice. You can either prostitute for me, or fight for me. What's it going to be?" the boss man asked and waited for an immediate answer.

Without hesitation, I told the man, "I will fight."

The man in the suit started to laugh. "How come whenever I give someone a choice between prostituting and fighting, yet only explain the details of prostituting, they always choose to fight? No one ever thinks to ask what it means to fight, they all just assume. You never know," the leader said, as he looked directly into my eyes, "you might have wanted to choose prostituting."

As much as I despised the man, he was right. I never thought to ask who or what I would have to fight or fight with. I just didn't want to be handled by another man like my father did to my sister. "Cut the tape around his legs and take him to his new home. Explain the rules and procedures around here. Make sure he knows them well," the big boss man instructed the muscle.

Chapter 8

Douglasville was a lower- middle-class suburban area. Most of the houses in Douglasville were built with the same structure with an appearance combining bricks and white vinyl sidings. Occasionally you saw a house that didn't fit and stood out amongst the others. For the most part, the neighbourhood was quiet, but the crime rate was higher in this area than most of the surrounding areas.

It was mid-afternoon when Detectives Seff and Jacobs pulled into the driveway of 15 Maplewood Road. There were no cars in the driveway and the house didn't have a garage. Even though all the signs told the detectives that no one was home, they still diligently left the car to make sure. The doorbell was broken so the detectives had no other choice but to knock. After several pounds on the door, the detectives officially concluded that no one was home to answer the door.

"Do you think we should look around back, maybe peek through an open window or something? You know, make sure everything is okay?" Detective Jacobs asked.

"I don't see why not," Detective Seff answered.

As the detectives made their way past the doorway, an old blue station wagon pulled up into the driveway. This hindered any plans of searching around back and attempting to discover criminal evidence against Kevin Mason. A woman exited the car clenching a grocery bag in one hand, and an oversized purse in the other. The detectives didn't waste any time introducing themselves by dropping their names and flashing their badges.

"So, you guys here to tell me you found my brother?" the woman questioned, as she made her way over to the detectives.

"I wasn't aware he was lost," Detective Seff replied. "We were actually hoping to talk to him."

"You sons of bitches," the woman said vulgarly. "What do you mean you weren't aware he was lost? I filed a missing persons report three days ago." Police cutbacks, an abundance of outstanding cases, processing paperwork delays, deficient technology, or just lack of funding were several typical reasons the detectives were unaware their main suspect has been declared missing for three whole days. And the last thing a person who took the time to file a report at a police station wants to hear from a law enforcement agent is an excuse as to why they are unknowing. However, Detective Seff isn't about making excuses; he's about stepping up to the plate and taking accountability.

"Ma'am, we didn't know your brother was missing, but we are looking for him. And if you don't mind answering some questions, we might be able to find him quicker," Seff steadfastly said. "Do you think you could help us?"

The woman shook her head up and down and replied, "All right, but only if you and your partner help take the rest of the groceries out of the backseat of my car."

Detective Jacobs and Seff each grabbed a couple of grocery bags and brought them inside the house. After the detectives brought the bags into the kitchen, the woman introduced herself as Diana Rodriguez and explained that Kevin Mason was her foster brother. Diana has a five-year-old son named Travis. Travis' father lives in Georgia and wants nothing to do with them. She currently works at a twenty-four hour convenience store at night, and cleans houses on the weekend for extra money. Kevin helps her pay the mortgage, and some of the expenses that come from raising a five-year-old child.

"So if you're not looking for Kevin because of the missing person's report I filed, then why are you looking for him?" Diana asked.

"We need to ask him a few questions about where he was last night," Detective Jacobs answered.

"Why, you think he did something?"

"Before we go into that, Ms. Rodriguez, to your knowledge, has Kevin ever been to St. Paul's Church located on Dunlap Street, about ten minutes west of here?" Seff inquired.

MOLECH

"Well, yeah, we all go there every Sunday unless Kevin and I both have to work." Confused and curious as to the reasoning behind the detective's question, Diana asked, "What does that have to do with finding my brother?"

"I'm sorry, Ms. Rodriguez, just one more question before I answer yours," the detective responded. "Being that you and your brother have attended St. Paul's Church many times, how well would you say your brother knows Father Thomas Michael?"

"He is our priest; we have been listening to his sermons for years. Kevin is very friendly with him. Sometimes they get together after the sermon and talk. Now what does this have to do with finding my brother?"

murder

"Father Michael's body was found murdered earlier this morning," Jacobs answered.

"We have reason to believe your brother might be connected to the killing. And his unknown whereabouts are not helping his case right now. Therefore, it's in his best interest that he resurfaces pretty damn quickly," Detective Seff concluded.

"You think Kevin killed Father Michael?" Diana said with a petty laugh in awe at the accusation. "He would never lay a finger on that man!"

"If you want to help your brother, start telling us places he might show up, his local hangouts, favourite places to eat, or any other place you can think of," Jacobs said, as he took out a pad and pen from his inside jacket pocket.

"Well, I don't know. My brother is a very private man. He never tells me where he goes, and I never ask."

"Listen, Ms. Rodriguez, as it stands, your brother is the only one right now that might be able to give us some answers that we need to solve this case. To be honest, it's

alibi – innocence

possible your brother has nothing to do with the priest's murder. But we can't dismiss any allegation until we question him and verify his ̖alibi.̗ So, if you are aware of even the slightest place your brother might show up, it would help," Seff pronounced, attempting to persuade Diana to provide them with a location.

"I don't know where he is and I can't tell you where he might be because I don't know. Otherwise, I would tell you."

"It sounds to me like you're protecting him, and if you are protecting him and your brother is guilty, then that would make you a co-conspirator to murder," Detective Jacobs declared. Raising his voice, he continued. "And do you know what would happen if you got charged as a co-conspirator? Well, besides going to jail, a social worker is going to come and take little Travis away. And you're going to lose your son for a very long time, if not for the rest of your life!" Jacobs said.

"Listen to me, Diana," Detective Seff interjected with a calm voice, breaking the harsh tone in the air. "Are you sure you can't tell us anything that might point us in the right direction of finding your brother?"

Diana didn't take threats well, but she knew her brother, and if her brother did commit the crime, she didn't want to go down with him; especially if it meant she would lose her only son. Travis was her life, losing him would mean she would lose everything. Diana has never been an inmate, although she has visited prison many times. Her father was serving a life sentence before he was stabbed to death by an opposing gang member.

Diana visited her father every weekend for fourteen years before he died. She really cared and loved him very much. However, the rules of prison didn't allow Diana and her father to have human contact unless it was through a glass barrier using a telephone. Every time she visited her father, it killed her to be so close, and not be able to hug or kiss him hello or goodbye. For fourteen years, Diana and her father left each other in tears. This was something Diana didn't want Travis to have to experience.

"I love my brother very much, but I can't risk losing Travis. I don't know where my brother is, but I could tell you something that might help your investigation."

"Go on, we're listening," Seff said.

"I met my brother when I was fifteen. We were placed in the same foster family around the same time. I connected with him pretty quickly and began to love him like he was family. He would look at me and tell me that I was a good person with a caring soul and that he would look after me as a brother should. Yet at the same time, he scared me. My brother claimed that he could hear voices that no one else could hear, and see images no one else could see. And when I asked him what these voices were telling him and what images he saw, he would speak of nothing but devilish things.

"There came a time where the voices and images were taking over his mind, and it became impossible for him to concentrate on anything else. So our foster parents took him to see a psychiatrist, and the doctor prescribed him medication that would suppress the voices in his head. It worked. As long as my brother took his pills, he was a normal person like everybody else. However, when he didn't take the medication, he became very violent. Now I know he wouldn't hurt me, just the evil people in this world he would always say. Still it scared me. I don't like violence and I don't want to see anyone get hurt."

Diana walked over to a shelf by the kitchen stove, grabbed a prescription bottle off it, and handed it to Detective Seff. "That's my brother's medication to suppress whatever evil he sees and hears in his head. He hasn't taken a pill since the day he disappeared. My brother isn't himself right now; you have to understand that. He's really not a bad person." Diana started to cry. "He takes care of Travis and me. Travis looks at him like a son would a father."

Seff looked at the label on the prescription bottle and learned the name of the doctor who prescribed the medicine,

Dr. Weinstein. "Diana, is Dr. Weinstein your brother's psychiatrist?"

"Yes."

"Do you have his address? We're going to need to speak with him."

"I have his business card somewhere, let me look for it."

"Do you mind if my partner and I look around your brother's bedroom while you find the address?"

"No, that's fine. He lives in the basement. It was the first door on your right when you first walked in."

Detective Seff and Jacobs walked down into the basement, which was no bigger than an average bedroom. The detectives thoroughly searched through Kevin's belongings, drawers, closet, and everywhere in between. However, they discovered nothing suspicious or any evidence that would connect him to the murder. Diana subsequently came down into the basement with Dr. Weinstein's business card and gave it to the detectives.

While in the basement, Seff's cell phone rang and it was Detective Garder. "David, there has been another murder and the captain wants you to meet him at the crime scene pronto."

"Is it the same MO as the priest's?" Seff asked, staring into Diana's eyes.

"Yeah, I'm afraid so."

"All right, let me call you back in just a moment for the location." Looking over at his partner, Seff informed Jacobs of the news. Soon after, they left Diana Rodriguez's home to meet Captain Baron at the new crime scene. However, before they departed, Seff convinced Diana to give them a recent photograph of her brother.

FOROGRAF

Chapter 9

10Q

My legs were free, but I couldn't run. I wouldn't even know where to run to. It didn't matter because I was being held by the same man I believe carried me into this place. The man had a strong grip around my arm, and kept aggressively pulling me in the direction he was moving. We were walking down a long corridor that had many doors. The corridor was old looking with rust, cracks, and holes everywhere you looked. There was water leaking from visible pipes, lights flickering, and guards with guns in their hands every ten feet. We turned down many corridors and walked up and down numerous flights of stairs. I kept thinking to myself, where am I? I begged myself to wake up from this awful nightmare, but this wasn't a nightmare, this was real. We finally stopped in front of a door that was labeled 10Q and the man began to speak.

"If you ever try to escape, you'll be lucky if we only decide to shoot you while you're unconscious. You will follow every order you're given and never question it. If you refuse to obey an order, you'll be living in a world of pain until you realise you should have obeyed the order. You are never to talk to anyone. Not me, not a guard, not another prisoner, no one. You'll get food and water when we bring it. If we forget to bring it, remember the rule that states you are never to talk to anyone.

"You chose to fight, so let me explain the rules of fighting here. You will fight when we tell you to fight. You'll be facing opponents younger, older, bigger, and smaller. In order to win a fight you must knock out your opponent or kill them. Sometimes you are given a weapon, but never the same weapon as your opponent. There is no referee, and there are certainly no rules. Now if you are injured and can no longer fight for us, you become a prostitute for however long we choose to keep you. If you win seven fights in a row, you go home and this place becomes a distant memory."

The muscle took a key out of his pocket and opened the door labeled 10Q. When the door opened and I was able to see inside, I became even more frightened than I was before. Inside Room 10Q were guards standing with machine guns. There were more than a dozen other male prisoners locked in small metal cages, no bigger than the ones you find at a dog kennel. I was hesitant to walk inside, so the man took me by the back of my neck and forcefully shoved me inside. He threw me into the door of an empty cage.

"Guard, unlock this cell," the muscle demanded. "We have a new fighter." The guard walked over to the cell door, relaxed his gun between his left arm and upper body, and took out a set of keys he kept in his right pocket. I wanted to grab the guard's gun and shoot my way out of here, but my hands weren't free and I didn't think I could overpower the guard or the ruthless man that brought me into the room. The guard unlocked the cage quickly and opened the door. The unkind man ordered me to enter the cell on my own, and out of fear of being more hurt than I already was, I complied with his demand. After I crawled into the cage, the guard subsequently closed and locked the door so I couldn't escape.

"Squeeze your hands through the food hole," the muscle demanded. After I complied once again, the guard took out a switchblade from his back pocket, and cut the tape around my wrists, freeing my arms from one another. "He is to get no food tonight, but if he behaves and follows all the rules, he could start receiving meals tomorrow."

"Yes, sir," the guard replied and returned to his post.

"Remember what I said, kid," the muscle said before he hit the cage door and then subsequently left the room.

Squashed inside a tiny cage with hardly any room to move, I tried to get as comfortable as I could, but there was no comfort in this place. I was able to see across from me, but my side views were blocked by thin panelling. Across from me was another boy. His weight, height, and age were hard to tell being that he was cramped into a small cell just like me. I tried not to stare at him, but I couldn't help it. In a way, I felt connected to him, since we were both in the same dilemma. It was obvious that he was trembling a great deal by the way his cage was rattling. My new neighbour and I weren't the only scared ones in this place; I could hear the sound of many other cages rattling as well.

Confined to a small cage by myself without the ability to speak or converse with anyone else, I started asking myself what was missing from this cage. There was no bed to sleep on, or a sink with running water, and there was no toilet to go to the bathroom. The floor of the cage had sizeable gaps so prisoners could release their bodily waste through them. Underneath the floor was another compartment that held a tray. On top of the tray were old newspapers, which were replaced when the harsh aroma from our bodily waste became too much for the guards to bear. I was being treated like an animal, but I had a feeling that was just what they wanted me to become.

At this point, I had no concept of time. The room had no windows so I couldn't tell whether it was day or night. I couldn't tell how long I had actually been locked up in this cage either. It was hard to sleep in such uncomfortable conditions, but I would manage to go in and out of consciousness, yet never for very long. Food eventually came, but it was typically old and rotten. The food was inedible, even for an animal. I mostly survived on water and moldy bread. Of course, I would eat around the mold.

The prisoner across from me wouldn't touch the food or even drink the water he was given. It made me think he had the right idea. Starving to death might be better than trying to survive in this place. But that particular death wouldn't come quick enough for me, or for the prisoner I call my neighbour.

The man in charge I encountered when I first came into this place entered 10Q wearing another expensive looking suit. He was accompanied by two guards holding major artillery. He ordered one of the 10Q guards to open the cage across from me. "Take him out of the cage and stand him up. It's his time to fight."

The prisoner slowly and nervously crawled out of the cage. When I got a good look at him, I could see he was no older than I was, and he was nothing but skin and bones. The guards that accompanied the boss man never took their guns off the young prisoner. The young boy was ordered to follow the man in the suit, but he was too weak to walk on his own, so the boss man had a guard drag him out of the room. I can't tell you exactly what happened to the poor boy between the time he left 10Q and the moment he returned, however, I can tell you that the boy returned the same way as he left, dragged by a guard. Only this time, the boy was being pulled by his feet while his head was being dragged on the ground leaving a trail of blood. It appeared as if something smashed the boy's skull right into his brain.

The boy was dead and dragged through 10Q for all the prisoners to see and then taken away into another room. It was a reality check for the prisoners. It was to let us know that death was a possible outcome and this was no joking matter. I wondered whom or what the boy fought since no other prisoner was taken out of 10Q. It also made me extremely nervous every time the door to this room opened because I was afraid it would be my time to fight. All of a sudden, the inside of this cage didn't feel so uncomfortable and I felt as long as I was inside this cage, I was safe from the unknown possibility of the death I could face outside of it.

I knew it would only be a matter of time before the 10Q door would open, and the man in the suit would enter and demand a guard to open my cage. Furthermore, I knew it was only a matter of time before it would be my turn to fight and stare death eye to eye. Seven other prisoners were chosen before the big boss man came for me. Five out of the seven prisoners came back through the 10Q door. However, they weren't alive to talk about their experience. I don't know

49

what happened to the other two; I never saw them again. New prisoners came in on a daily basis and they all shared the same look on their face: terrified, anxious, and worried. I'm sure my face was no different when I first entered.

I've been crammed in a cage for god knows how long. I'm not even sure if I have the strength to stand up or to throw any power behind a punch. It didn't matter. In this place, when it was your time, it was your time. Choices weren't a luxury a prisoner had because if it were up to us, we would all be breathing free air, miles and miles away from this place. Sometimes I could taste freedom at the tip of my tongue, but it was always overcome by the sour taste of imprisonment.

What kind of people were the individuals who held us here? What drove them to treat people the way they did? Whatever happened to their conscience? When did they lose the ability to reason with themselves? Why couldn't they see what they were really doing? Where did the good go inside their hearts?

"Guard, open this cage door," the boss man commanded, as he pounded on my cage. The touch of his hand against my cage sent shivers down my spine and fear throughout my body. The guard quickly ran over, took out his keys, and unlocked the cage door. I knew this was the point where the prisoner was supposed to crawl out of the cage, but I stayed still. The one in charge bent down, looked into the cage, and saw me trembling. "Now, son, this isn't the way to act before your big debut. Your opponent will see your fear a mile away and use it to his advantage. You want to be brave, son." He spoke to me just as my father would before he would beat me to a pulp.

The boss man could see that I did not intend to leave the cage, so he ordered the same guard who unlocked my cage to drag me out. The guard got on his hands and knees and placed his upper body into the cage. Then he took me by my feet and pulled me out. I tried gripping the cage through the gaps of the metal cage, but the guard was too powerful for me. As soon as I was out of the cage, the boss man stood me on my feet and surprisingly, I was able to hold myself up, but it hurt to stand up straight.

Just like all the other times when the man in the suit entered 10Q, he was escorted by two other men with sizeable weaponry. And just like all the other prisoners who left before me, the two men placed their guns only inches from my body. "Let's go," the boss man instructed, as he walked toward the door to 10Q. Most of my body ached from sitting in the same crouching position for so long, but I managed to follow the man in the suit. The two guards with the artillery followed shortly behind me with their guns pointing in my direction. When I exited 10Q, it was the last time I ever saw that room again.

drove an motivar
escorted- escolta.
CROUCHING- agochar

Chapter 10

After leaving Diana Rodriguez's house, Detective Seff and Jacobs got back into their squad car. However, just before Seff entered the car, he called Detective Garder at police headquarters for the location of the second murder. "The address of the crime scene is 16 Canton Street in Troy," Garder informed him. Seff was not that familiar with the Troy area, so he immediately typed the location into his navigational system. They were about thirty minutes from the crime scene, yet they were hoping to make it there in twenty.

"David, I was able to track down the file on Jake Weans, but you're not going to like what I have to tell you," Garder disclosed. "Since the case file was over twenty-five years old, it was moved into a storage room in the basement of the fourth precinct. Unfortunately, three years ago a water pipe broke and flooded the basement, destroying many of the records. However, a lot of the files were saved, but not the one on our suspect. So the file is forever gone."

"That's just great," Detective Seff responded sarcastically. "Is there anything else you want to tell me that might cheer me up?"

"I called the sanitation office where Kevin Mason works like you asked, and they said he hasn't been at work in the last three days."

"Then I would say he is officially missing."

"Agreed, also, Dr. Sachs from the medical lab faxed over a couple of photographs of the symbol carved into the back of Father Michael's body. A group of us are trying to figure out what it might mean, but we haven't had any luck yet."

"Well, keep trying and hopefully someone will come up with something. Is there anything else?"

"That's it for now."

"Okay, I'll touch base with you later."

"All right, let me know if you need anything."

"Will do."

The detectives arrived at 16 Canton Street in a little over twenty-three minutes. Troy was a town of upper-class, wealthy citizens in an area that had its own privately trained security force patrolling the neighbourhoods at all hours of the night. However, the killer was able to enter their turf, undetected, and murder someone they were hired to protect. In front of the home where the murder took place, news affiliates were making a crowd. It always puzzled Detective Seff how reporters were sometimes quicker to a crime scene than a cop was.

The dead body was located in the backyard of the victim's home. The property was a little more than two acres of land with the house situated in the middle of the property. Police officers were scattered throughout the property looking for evidence. Before the detectives made their way to the backyard, they spotted Captain Baron talking with a couple of uniformed police officers on the front porch of the house. The detectives thought it would be best to talk to him first before they visited the scene of the crime.

"Captain, sorry to interrupt your conversation, but we got here as soon as we heard," Seff said.

Captain Baron excused the uniformed officers so he could talk privately to the detectives. Captain Baron seemed calm and stress free, but he was anything but tranquil. "Well, tell me you got a lead or something on the killer. The son of a bitch has to be stopped! This story is only moments from hitting the information highway and I don't want this jerk thinking he's a celebrity. I don't need to tell you that having a serial killer roaming the streets that we're supposed to protect makes us look bad. Not to mention it's giving me heartburn and a bad case of diarrhoea. And I don't like having a burning sensation from my ass, so tell me you have something that we can go on."

Captain Baron was a very serious person, and he wasn't kidding about the heartburn or diarrhoea. He was carrying

53

acid reducer tablets in the left front hand pocket of his pants. "Sir, I think we have a pretty good lead. Your friend, Irving Adelson, pointed us in the direction of a man named Jake Weans who had committed murder with the same MO about thirty years ago. We learned he changed his name to Kevin Mason and presently lives ten minutes away from where the first killing took place."

"And a half hour away from here," Jacobs added.

"We went to visit Mr. Mason at his latest residency, only he wasn't there, but we did get to speak with his foster sister," Seff continued. "His foster sister's name is Diana Rodriguez and she informed us that her brother went missing three days ago and she even filed a missing person's report. She also told us that Kevin regularly attends the St. Paul's Church and routinely conversed with Father Michael. But that's not the best part. His sister also informed us that Kevin takes medication to suppress strange voices and images in his head. If he doesn't take his medication, he becomes violent. Kevin Mason hasn't taken his medication since the day he vanished."

"So we have a suspect, but we don't know where he is?" Captain Baron pondered.

"Yeah, but we have a recent picture of him, and a giant distribution centre," Detective Seff said, gesturing toward the crowd of reporters.

Captain Baron took the picture from the detectives and said, "I'll go share this picture with the press. I'll keep it short and only state that we're looking for this man for questioning in relation to the current murders, but nothing else. You two go to the backyard and look over the crime scene. After I talk to the press, I'll come join you in the backyard and we'll talk about where we go from here."

"Yes sir," the detectives said simultaneously. While the captain walked over to the press to make his speech, the detectives made their way to the backyard. The corpse was situated on the grass under a leafless tree. However, the body wasn't fully attached. The killer had detached the arms and legs from the victim, yet put the appendages back in their rightful place. Furthermore, the killer positioned the body like Jesus on the cross; arms out to the side with his feet crossed. A forensic team was still taking Polaroids of the body and searching the surrounding area for clues.

"Why do you think he shoots them in the eyes?" Detective Jacobs asked Seff while they were standing over the body.

"Well, besides the obvious of hindering the victims' ability to identify the killer in a line up, my best guess is that our killer is a religious man. And like many religious people, he believes that the eyes are the pathway to the soul. Therefore, by shooting each victim in the eyes, the killer believes he's somehow extinguishing their souls. The killer did position the victim's body like Jesus on the cross."

"Yeah, but the killer also murdered a priest. What kind of religious man kills a priest?" Jacobs retorted.

"Maybe he's a Jew for Jesus," Seff replied.

After the forensic photographer was finished taking pictures of the dead body, Detective Seff turned the body onto its side. It was then he discovered that there was a blotchy stain of blood seeping through the lower part of the victim's shirt. Subsequently, Seff pulled up the victim's shirt and revealed the same bloody marking as the one carved in Father Michael's back.

While the detectives were looking over and studying the victim's body, the officer who first arrived at the crime scene walked over to the detectives. "How are you doing, fellas? I'm Officer Dixon, the primary officer at the crime scene. Captain Baron told me to find you, and inform you of what I was able to gather about the victim, and today's events."

"Well, it would be appreciated," Jacobs responded.

Before the officer told the detectives what he knew, he waited for Detective Jacobs to take out his pen and pad from his jacket pocket. "Well, the victim's name is Mark Keller, age fifty-two. He was discovered by his wife shortly after she entered the house."

"You spoke to the wife?" Jacobs asked.

"Yes, sir, I did," Dixon responded.

"What's her alibi?" Seff inquired.

"Well, she stated that she was in Florida all week visiting their daughter. She was expecting her husband to pick her up at the airport this morning, but he never showed up. Eventually, she got tired of waiting, so she had a taxi drive her home. After the taxi dropped her off, she opened her front door and immediately noticed a trail of blood leading from the basement door, past the sliding doors in the kitchen, and into the backyard. She immediately ran outside and discovered her husband's dead body. Then she ran back inside the house and called nine-one-one."

"Did you ask her if her husband had any enemies that would want to hurt him?" Seff asked.

"Yes, it was the second question I asked," Dixon declared. "She said no. She could not even imagine why someone would want to hurt him."

"Did she tell you what Mr. Keller did for a living?"

"Yes, he was a partner of an accounting firm called Littman, Bowen and Keller. It's located thirty-five minutes from here in Raceda."

"Is there anything else?" Seff inquired.

"That's about it. I also spoke to the private security patrol, but they didn't see anything." *felicitorlo*

"All right, good work," Detective Seff praised. "Now I'm going to need you to grab some of the other officers and canvas the area, ask some of the nearby residents if they saw or heard anything relating to the murder, or anything suspicious that might seem relevant."

"Not a problem, I'll get right on it sir." → *yame pongo ahacerla*

"All right, get back to me as soon as possible."

Soon after Officer Dixon left on Seff's instructions, Captain Baron walked over to the detectives. "Gentlemen, the word is out. Kevin Mason's picture should have been displayed all over Philadelphia as of four minutes ago,"

Captain Baron said, staring, at his watch. "Did you speak to Officer Dixon?"

"Yes sir Captain, we did," Seff responded. "I just had him grab a couple of officers to canvas the area."

"Good." Suddenly the captain noticed the small bloodstain on the victim's shirt. "What is that?"

"What is what, sir?" Jacobs asked.

"The man was shot in his eyes and chest. Why is there a bloodstain protruding through the lower portion of his shirt?"

"It's a stain from the marking the killer engraved in his back," Seff answered. "Father Michael had a similar one."

"Why am I hearing about this marking now and not before?" the captain asked heatedly, expecting an immediate response.

"It must have slipped my mind, Captain," Seff replied.

"See that it doesn't happen again! I want to be informed about every little detail of this case. Is that understood?" Captain Baron yelled.

"Yes, sir," both Detective Seff and Jacobs answered concurrently.

"It doesn't matter though; no one knows what the marking means. Detective Garder, amongst others, had been trying to decipher it for the past hour or so, but were having no such luck. It's nothing more than a link right now. Even the detectives thirty years ago couldn't figure out what the markings engraved in the victims meant; as per your old acquaintance that is. Chances are we won't either without the killer deciphering it for us."

"Well, I like to think police intelligence is a little better than it was thirty years ago," the captain quickly responded and paused at the sight of two men in suits walking over to them. "Listen, this case is getting to be more than the two of you can handle. I pulled two other detectives onto the case, but they'll work under your command. Therefore, they'll report to you, and you'll report to me," Captain Baron said, speaking directly at Detective Seff. "We're borrowing two

57

detectives from another precinct for now because we're a little low on manpower and they have a few to spare."

The two men in suits finally made it over to where the captain and detectives were standing. They introduced themselves as Detective Ronald and Russ. It just so happens that they were both rookie detectives, however, they had many years of police work under their belt. The captain informed the rookies of the chain of command, and left the crime scene to go back to police headquarters where they would meet later. Detective Seff updated Ronald and Russ with the details of the current investigation, and decided it would be best if they visited Mark Keller's place of work, Littman, Bowen and Keller. In the meantime, Seff and Jacobs would pay a visit to Kevin Mason's psychiatrist, Dr. Weinstein.   SAIKAIATRES

"When you get to the accounting firm, try to talk to a partner or someone high on the corporate ladder. If you can't, talk to whoever will talk to you," Seff instructed the rookies. "Find out if Mr. Keller had any enemies or if they know of any reason why someone would want to kill him. Also, try to find out if the accounting firm has some connection with Kevin Mason. Maybe he's a client of theirs or worked for them at some point in the past.

"Before you go, it might be a good idea to check the police records to see if the accounting firm has been under investigation for anything. You should also contact the Better Business Bureau and find out if anyone has made any complaints about them, too. That type of information sometimes comes in handy before you start investigating a company. It just might lead you in the right direction. If you discover anything pertinent, call me on my cell phone, if not, I will see you back at the station."

Detective Seff did not like bossing other people around. He never saw himself as a leader or someone people should look up to. However, the people who knew him best thought differently.

After the detectives parted, they headed toward their planned destinations. On the way to see Dr. Weinstein, Seff called Detective Garder at the station house and instructed her to find out any information she could on Mark Keller, but more specifically, a reason why someone would want him dead.

Chapter 11

What Lies Beyond 10Q

I was taken through the same horrible looking corridors that brought me to the room labelled 10Q, but I could not remember for sure if it was the same route. We eventually stopped in front of another door labelled 3F. There were two guards standing side by side in front of the door, making it impossible to enter. The guards did not move until the man in the suit instructed them with his hand. The boss man then reached into his inside jacket pocket and pulled out a shiny gold key which he used to open 3F.

When the door opened, the man in the suit entered and I was instructed by one of the guards to enter as well, so I did. The two guards who were following me entered right after and shut the door behind them. Room 3F was an empty, tiny looking room; however, there was another door, but it was closed. I also noticed a video camera hanging just above the door. The boss man stopped walking just before the other door and slowly turned around.

"Behind this door awaits your future," the man in charge said. "When it opens, you will enter it on your own. I know you're probably scared. I won't lie to you, most individuals are, but it would be in your best interest to concentrate on the fight and not your fear. Trust me when I say your opponent is thinking of one thing, and one thing only, to tear your head from your neck and make sure you never get up."

I was scared and I was shaking, but the man in the suit was right. I was about to fight for my life, I should concentrate on what matters most and not my fear. "Now son, I'm going to let you in on a little secret. If you win tonight, I won't send you back to that awful cage you have been locked in for days. If you win, you'll be resting on a nice comfortable bed. You'll also have your very own bathroom with a shower, sink, and toilet. Now I bet that sounds nice, but it gets even better. I will even have my personal chef make you a delicious, juicy steak, with the tastiest mashed potatoes you will ever eat."

Just the mention of a juicy steak made my stomach growl. It made me think about the last time I actually had a real meal. "However, you should also know this; if you lose to your opponent, he will get everything I just offered you. And remember, you are no good to me injured, so if you can't fight, then you prostitute for me because if you're injured or not, my customers won't care." The man in the suit looked at his shimmering gold watch. "Now that door is going to open in about three minutes, so you better start thinking about what you're going to do when it does. You'll be fighting hand to hand combat tonight. There will be no weapons.

"Now I'm almost positive that deep down inside, you really hate me," the boss man said, as he started to tie a blue armband around my bicep. "And I'm here to tell you that you will never get a chance to take that anger out on me. So if I were you, I would take all that anger and hatred out on your opponent tonight. If it makes you feel better to think of my face on your adversary, so be it. Now this is the last time we will ever meet, so good luck to you."

The man in the suit left 3F the same way he entered, but the guards never moved. They stayed pointing their weapons in my direction. Most likely to make sure I entered through the mysterious door when it opened. I knew in my head that I shouldn't concentrate on my nervousness, but it was something I couldn't help. The thunderous sound of my heart beating at a rapid pace made it hard for me to concentrate on anything else. Suddenly the door opened and a deafening sound rang through my ears.

It was the noise coming from the arena. From what I could tell, the battleground wasn't that large, but there was enough room to run around. The arena was really just four cement walls and a wooden floor. There were people standing around, but above about two floors up. The audience was screaming and yelling two different colours, the colour of the band around my arm, and the band colour around the arm of my opponent.

From a short distance, I could see my opponent moving fast toward me, but I was too frightened to move. Suddenly, I was pushed from behind and thrown into the arena barely a foot away from my opponent. He was wearing a red armband around his right arm in which he swung at my face leading with his fist; I barely got out of the way. Unexpectedly, the doors to the arena closed, creating no means of escape.

My enemy would not stop throwing his fists at my head, throwing punch after punch. He kept missing though and was hitting nothing but air. However, my opponent managed to chase me into a corner, and it was in there where he landed his first punch. I held my arms in the air trying to protect my face, but he threw a roundhouse punch and nailed me on the side of my head. His next punch landed as well. Nevertheless, I managed to stay on my feet and keep my hands up.

My adversary's punches did two things. It first reminded me of my father when he hit me. Yet the force behind my father's punches were a lot more powerful. Second, my opponent's punches put an end to my nervousness and my fear metamorphosed into adrenalin. I could feel myself changing as if I had grown three inches taller, forty pounds heavier, and a lot angrier. My opponent could have landed thirty punches and I doubt it would have fazed me one bit.

I pushed my opponent back and forced my way out of the corner. I could tell he was tired from his uncontrollable heavy breathing. He was also moving a lot slower than he was before. His punches became predictable and eventually, so were his every movement; that was when I took over the fight. My first punch knocked him back two steps and made his nose bleed in one nostril. I punched him again in the same exact spot, and blood just started to pour. The punch fazed him, so I took advantage and tackled him to the ground.

muvmens — movement

I placed myself on top of him, and he immediately tried to push me off, but he didn't have enough strength to do it. His arms were like branches flopping in the wind just barely holding on. I began to punch his face without any self-control. It was as if my consciousness did not exist. Blood was pouring not only from his nose now, but his mouth, right eye, and from the side of his forehead. If I could have stopped I would have, but something inside of me prevented any such action. It was not until I realised my opponent was dead that I stopped. It was then I realised that I became the vicious animal this cold-hearted place trained me to be.

There was enough blood from my opponent on me to think I was gushing blood myself, but I was not even hurt in the least bit. The crowd never stopped cheering, for this behaviour turned them on. They kept chanting the color blue repeatedly, as if I was a king or a champion. I did not exactly know how to feel about the situation, but I kept my head down toward the floor. Suddenly, my opponent's side door opened, and there stood a man I have never seen before. He was dressed in black and there were two guards with guns standing behind him. The man dressed in black had very unique characteristics, but the one that stood out the most was his spiky, bright blond hair. He rolled his fingers at me as a command to come to him. I walked over, but I took my time getting there.

As soon as I walked through the door, it closed automatically and the two guards with guns pointed them in my face. The room was identical to 3F, tiny with two doors on opposite ends. "That was an excellent fight, very bloody impressive," the man dressed in black said with an Australian accent. At least I thought it was Australian. "Follow me and don't try anything funny or my friends here will shoot your face off." We left the room and into a hallway. This hallway was not like the other corridors I have seen in this place. This hallway was painted nicely with beautiful paintings hanging on the wall. There were no visible pipes or rusted spots. The floor was even carpeted.

"Welcome to the other side of the organisation," the man in black said animatedly. "You could say it's a little brighter. I was told you were promised a room with a nice bed, a bathroom with a shower and toilet, and the best meal of your life. Well, don't you worry about it; I'm going to take care of that for you. You've done real well for yourself tonight. You've won yourself a nice place to recuperate, and some grub you'll actually want to sink your teeth into. I'm also here to tell you, my friend, this could possibly be just the beginning of the many prizes you can win.

"You thought coming into this place was a bad thing, but when you walk out of here you might think differently. I'm talking about a lot of money in your pocket and electronics you can't buy on the market." Blondie stopped walking and turned to me so we were face to face. "You might be too young to understand this, but with your fighting skills, we might have done you a favour by bringing you into this place. I think you have a chance to be a winner." Then the man in black took out a key and opened the door to my right. "This will be your new room for now."

Chapter 12

Detective Seff and the rest of the detectives who were working on the case, eventually made it back to police headquarters around eight thirty in the evening. When all members of the task force were present, they got together to meet in Captain Baron's office. There they shared and discussed all the information they were able to obtain from their assigned tasks.

The conference was necessary, but seemed futile to each of the attendees since the detectives didn't obtain any useful information. Rookie detectives Ronald and Russ couldn't find any connection between the accounting firm and the death of Mark Keller. Littman, Bowen and Keller, is a well run accounting firm with no history of any illegal or malicious activities. Furthermore, they couldn't find a link between the accounting firm and Kevin Mason.

Detective Garder wasn't able to discover any reason for the killing of Mark Keller. She was only able to uncover how caring of a man he was. Every year Mr. Keller donated over sixty thousand dollars to different charities. He also taught two college classes free of charge. And in between his work and teaching, Mr. Keller volunteered at a clinic for the deaf.

Detective Seff and Jacobs didn't get anywhere with Kevin Mason's psychiatrist, Dr. Weinstein. He answered every question with the same three words, "Doctor/Client privilege." As long as Kevin Mason wasn't officially declared dead, Dr. Weinstein wouldn't talk about his patient with anyone. There were no more paths to follow, there were no leads to pursue, and the investigation had come to a standstill. There were only the markings left in the victims' bodies, but they were pieces to a puzzle that didn't fit.

It was a few minutes past 11 P.M. and Detective Seff was sitting in the lounge where the officers came to relax on their breaks. The lounge was quiet with only the thirteen-inch television hanging in the corner of the room making any noise. The television was old and was only capable of displaying one channel clearly, which was an all day news channel. Seff was sitting on a ripped up leather couch with his feet up on a wooden coffee table held up by four cement cinderblocks. He was taking a short break from trying to decode the meaning behind the markings carved into the victims' bodies. While the detective was resting, a story about today's events came on the news.

"Today's top story is a sad and terrifying one. Two dead bodies were found murdered in cold blood only hours apart from each other. One of the men was the well-known Father Thomas Michael, most famous for his valiant efforts to fight poverty in the Pittsburgh area, and the other, a loving husband and father who went by the name Mark Keller. Our on the scene news reporter, Jackie Hussein, was able to talk with Mark Keller's neighbour earlier today. This is what she had to say about the victim."

"Mark Keller was my neighbour for twelve years. He was a kind and gentle man, who would never hurt a soul. He would always be willing to lend a helping hand whenever someone needed it. Mark was a person you could depend on and talk to when troubles arose. I don't understand what kind of person would hurt a man like that. I just can't believe this happened."

"Both men were killed in the same gruesome fashion. As of now, police have not made any arrests or named a suspect responsible for the killings. However, they are looking for a man for questioning. He goes by the name of Kevin Mason. The Pittsburgh police department is asking if anyone sees this person, or have seen this person in the past three days, to please contact your local police department, or call this telephone hotline, 1-800-555-TIPS."

"Don't worry; tomorrow Kevin Mason's face will be on the cover of every newspaper across the state. He's not going to be able to hide for very long," the captain said. Captain Baron and Detective Seff were typically the last two officers to leave at night. The two of them called it dedication; however, other people might call it a lack of a social life. "I'm working on obtaining a sizable amount of reward money for information leading to the arrest of the killer. If someone is harbouring him, he or she won't be for very long. Why don't you go home, it looks like you can use a shower and some sleep."

"I'm not tired, this case is just frustrating me. We have two murders, one suspect who we cannot locate, not to mention we don't have any real evidence connecting him to the murders or any reason why he would want to kill them. And I'm stuck here with my tail between my legs not able to do a damn thing about it."

"Frustration isn't going to solve this case, and it's only going to slow you down. There is nothing you or I can do about it now, except hope the killer makes a mistake, or some new information comes to light."

"So you're saying there is nothing we can do except wait for the killer to strike again. That's what you're saying?"

"I hate to say it, but yes, right now all we can do is wait," Captain Baron responded.

"You're right; I just don't want to face the truth. The killer is good and it's pissing me off."

"I understand that in all your years as a detective, you have never been put in this type of situation before. It's a hard thing to accept, but it is reality. I remember my first time something like this happened. There was some guy raping women all over town, leaving no evidence of his identity. There was nothing I could do but wait for him to strike again and leave a clue or get caught trying. I kept thinking of another poor woman being lurked upon and then forcibly raped. It's a hard thing to take, but it was reality and it was something I had to face, just as you have to face this now. So go home, get some rest. I'm not asking it's an order, Detective."

"All right, I'm going home. I'll pick up where I left off in the morning."

"Grab your jacket. I'll wait and we'll leave together."

Chapter 13 ✓

Scarred for Life - The Journey Comes to an End

The room to where I was brought was exquisite. A palace compared to my last lodgings. This was a room you only see in magazines built for the wealthiest people of society. The top of the bed was covered in a canopy and the mattress was outlined with a gold frame. The walls were covered in scenic paintings and large mirrors. The floor was half-carpeted and half-covered with smooth tile. "As you can see we take good care of our winners here. Go inside and take a look." I walked inside the room and only the man dressed in black followed me in. The room was everything I said it was, and very pleasing. The bathroom was just as beautiful. The shower was quite large with three showerheads. There was also a whirlpool bathtub located adjacent to the shower. They even hung a white bathrobe and a pair of slippers for me to use.

"In the top drawer under the sink you will find all the toiletries you will need and below that drawer are your towels. Nice and soft like mine. On top of your bed, you will find we put new clothes for you to wear. Since we didn't know your exact size, you'll find the same articles of clothing in different sizes. Pick the one that fits you best, and leave the rest on the floor. Someone will come around and pick them up.

"For now, this is your room. What you do with your time in this room is your own business. But my advice to you is to rest up, but to also train. Your next fight is in three days, so don't get too comfortable. Your food will be here in two hours." The man dressed in black started to leave through the door, but he turned around at the doorway. "Oh yeah, there will be at least one guard standing by your door at all times. Also, above me, you will find a camera. Keep in mind someone is always watching you, so don't try anything funny." Blondie then left the room and shut the door behind him. The door locked automatically.

My tremors temporarily seemed to vanish, for this room made me feel like I was in another place. It was like being in a hotel room on a vacation from life. However, the camera by the door made me a little nervous. I didn't like being watched. What if there were other cameras in this room, hidden where the eyes can't see?

I looked at myself in the mirror for the first time in days. My face looked like it was covered in red war paint. The dark colour of my opponent's blood made my eyes stand out above the rest of my facial features. After I took off my shirt, I could see that my weight loss was noticeable. I was skin and bones to begin with, now it seemed as if I was just bones. I know the mirror doesn't lie, but it was hard to recognise the person I saw.

I started running the shower water and positioned the valve so the water came out warm. I took off all my clothes but my underwear, just in case they were watching. The water sprinkling from the three showerheads felt so refreshing against my body I think I spent almost an hour just standing there with no movement. I watched the dry blood slowly trickle down my body and gradually into the shower drain. I stood motionless and dazed, mesmerised by who I have become.

After my long shower, I put on the white bathrobe they left hanging on the door. Although it was a little too big, it was soft and comfortable. I found my way to the bed and just collapsed on top of the clothes they wanted me to wear. It felt like an eternity from the last time I was able to lay down, especially on a mattress so soft and pleasing. It didn't take but a few seconds before I drifted into sleep.

I was awoken a short time afterward by another man I have never seen before. I called him the Waiter. This man never spoke to me; he would only wheel in the food and leave. It was the meal promised to me by the man in the suit, steak with mashed potatoes. The Waiter didn't leave any silverware for me to use, and I couldn't ask for some. They expected me to eat the food with my hands like a barbarian, so I did. All the times the Waiter brought me something to eat he never once brought me silverware.

I really only did four things in the room: slept, ate, showered, and shadowboxed. I would say that out of the four I slept the most, even though it wasn't easy. I didn't dream, I had nightmares every time. It was usually the same nightmare repeatedly. The nightmare takes place inside the arena where I beat my first opponent. I can't see the crowd, but I can hear them chanting a colour. The only person I could see is the one I'm fighting.

My opponent is a little bigger than I am, but not by much. Throughout the nightmare, he is constantly taunting me with words of dishonour and humiliation. I want to hurt him really bad, but I can't. In the nightmare, every movement I try to make was carried out in slow motion. Even when I was able to hit him, it didn't even faze him. He just smiles and laughs at my power and capacity to fight. After several laughs, my adversary starts to punish my face with his fists and eventually do the same to my body. I typically wake up in the middle of the beating in a terrible sweat accompanied by heavy breathing.

Time went by quickly because it wasn't long until I was taken back to the tiny room which led to the fighting arena. Two armed guards came to my luxurious room and escorted me. Blondie was waiting for me inside the room, sitting on a chair with a small brown box in his hand. "Hey, I hope the last two days for you have been comfortable, and you're all rested for your second match." Blondie suddenly picked himself up from the chair, but left the brown box on the floor.

"Come sit down; relax a little while I talk to you." I did as he said and quietly sat in the chair. As soon as I sat down, he wrapped a red ribbon around my arm and stepped back. "I know exactly what you're thinking, what am I going to win after I beat my opponent to smithereens. Well, it's a surprise, but I assure you it's going to feel real good against your skin." It wasn't exactly what I was thinking. My thoughts were actually focused on what lies ahead of me on the other side of the arena door.

"We don't have too much time because in about two minutes the door to the arena is going to open, and you know what you're going to have to do. I'm here to tell you, this fight is going to be a little different than your last." Different didn't sound good and hearing those words made me nervous. "You're each going to battle with a weapon.

"Your weapon is located in the brown box next to you by your feet. Why don't you go ahead and pick up the box." I reached down by my feet and picked up the brown box. The box wasn't heavy and I could hear something rattling inside. "As you've probably noticed there is a combination lock on it. The lock can be opened by a three digit code. You enter the combination by turning the dial on the lock clockwise, counterclockwise, and then clockwise again.

"Now listen very carefully. I am not going to give you the combination to the lock. However, I am going to tell you where you can find it. The combination can be found on a very visible red banner hanging above your opponent's door," Blondie said, looking at his watch. "You only have thirty seconds, so if I was you, I would stand up and get ready. It's your time to shine. Good luck, mate!" Then the man in black left, shutting the door behind him.

I instantly got up from the chair and stood in front of the arena door. I was shaking so badly I was making the object inside the box rattle. Without warning, the arena door flew open and the match began. As soon as the door opened I saw two things, but I only paid attention to one of them. I saw my opponent run out into the arena and drop to the ground with a case of his own. I also saw the red banner above my opponent's door with the combination I needed to open the box. I paid attention to the combination of the box.

I quickly memorised the combination and dropped to the floor to open the box. I kept repeating the combination in my

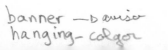

banner → D aviso
hanging → colgor

RATTLE — Songera
sonar, agitar,
golpear

head, 2, 24, 29. When I dropped to the floor, I couldn't hear anything, but the repetition of the combination in my head. I turned the dial as fast as I could, clockwise, counterclockwise, and clockwise again. My first attempt was unsuccessful and I didn't open the box. However, I didn't get frustrated, only more nervous. I had two enemies at this point, my opponent and time.

I tried again 2, 24, 29 and the box instantly jumped open. Inside the box was a shining blade with a round blunt handle. I quickly picked it up out of the box, and turned to my opponent but it was too late. I turned right into the blunt end of a bat held by my adversary. He hit me right on the top of my forehead and split my skin in two. I went out quicker than a light bulb. I don't believe my opponent used the bat on me more than once because I didn't have any other cuts or bruises except for the one on my forehead.

After the fight, I only remember glimpses of the next couple of hours. I'm surprised I remember anything at all because of the severe concussion I received from the fight. I remember being dragged down unsanitary hallways and being thrown on a bed. I remember being violently stripped of all my clothes and having my wrists and ankles chained to the bed, so I was facedown with my arms and legs spread. I even recall a mask being put over my face and the taste of metal in my mouth. And then there was this touch I remember vividly.

It started on my leg and ran all the way up to my fingers. It was the hand of a sadistic man. I know not because he raped me, but because when he touched the palm of my hand with his fingers, something unusual happened. I was able to see detailed images of that man's entire past. The visions of his life became as real to me as if I lived it myself. His name was Anthony Flormont. But not only was I able to see his past, I was able to see the lives of all of whom he ever encountered.

Anthony was a sick, perverted, overweight man. He had touched many boys before, in ways that are forbidden by law.

73

He also had a wife and a newborn baby boy. He was evil, and I was about to be his next victim. I said my first words in the establishment to him. I know I was breaking one of the cardinal rules, but I thought to myself what kind of punishment could be any worse than where this situation was leading. With all my strength, I said his name, "Anthony Flormont," hoping to strike fear that I could identify him. I don't think he heard me, though; I hardly heard the words myself. There were sounds of gunfire coming from the hallway. It was so loud, it was almost impossible to hear anything else. On the other hand, the hail of gunfire must have scared the middle-aged man because he jumped back and quickly rushed to gather his things and put his clothes back on.

The sounds of gunfire happened to be a shootout between the guards and the New York City police department. I was actually kidnapped and brought twenty feet away from where the four men in the van picked me up. I guess they drove me around in circles for a long time, so I wouldn't be able to pinpoint the radius of their location. It wound up that this hell forsaken place was an abandoned hotel, deserted by its original owners in 1983. It was sold to a dummy corporation and made into a pool of illegal activities.

Many arrests were made, but the main players behind the illegitimate scheme left in body bags. Two police officers died that day as well. The man who was about to rape me was arrested and eventually put in prison. The police discovered three rooms full of adolescent prisoners locked in cages like the one I was placed in. They even found an eight-year-old boy chained to a bed as they found me, except he had been dead for many days.

A police officer, whose name I do not know, found me, covered me up with a blanket, and removed the mask covering my face. The metal I tasted came from a zipper located by the mouth of the mask. I was eventually unchained and taken to a hospital in an ambulance. It took fourteen stitches to close the gash on my forehead. A doctor took an

MRI of my head to make sure there weren't any internal problems. He couldn't find anything wrong, but he did notice something unusual about my brain. "To explain it simply," the doctor said, "where most people use ten percent of their brain, it looks like you use close to ninety."

Even though my brain did not suffer from any injury, the strike of the bat against my forehead left me with a very visible scar. The police detective who stayed with me at the hospital told me I was lucky to be alive. They found over fifteen dead bodies of children about my age. The detective also told me that I had some explaining to do. You see, when I was in and out of consciousness, the police were able to discover my real name and eventually tied me to the murder of my father. I told the detective the truth and informed him about the abuse my sister and I had taken. How my father molested his own daughter and physically beat his own son. The detective believed me, but it was probably my vast medical record of broken bones and bruises that convinced him. With no living relatives alive to take care of me, and since I was too young to take care of myself, I was placed into foster care.

On the other hand → al mismo tiempo?

GATHER - coger agarror

Kidnapped → Kitnopt - secuestrado

Chapter 14

Detective Seff often worked late into the night, however, he never knew for sure if it was his dedication to the job or something else. Being part of the police force was something David Seff always wanted to do, yet he knew life was more than just working a job. Unfortunately, for Seff, he was never too proficient with the other parts of life. Most of the time, he used work as an excuse to take his mind off his life of solitude. To make matters worse, Seff was also an insomniac. Sleep never came easily to him, even as a little kid. No matter how hard the detective would try to drift into a world of unconsciousness, he consistently tossed and turned in his bed for most of the night.

Leaving work at an early hour was never pleasurable for him. Years of coming home to an empty apartment were like putting salt on an open wound, a constant reminder of the loneliness life has to offer. Therefore, instead of going home to an empty apartment, tossing and turning for most of the night, Seff frequently went to a bar called The Rum Shaker. The Rum Shaker was located only two blocks away from his apartment, which was very convenient for the detective. The majority of the staff was on a first name basis with him, and knew the detective quite well. Since tonight was no different from any other, Seff stopped at The Rum Shaker for a drink before going home.

The Rum Shaker was moderately sized with a long bar, and a seating area of tables and booths. It was Friday night so the establishment was busier than usual. Yet, Seff was able to find an empty stool at the bar. Two bartenders worked at The Rum Shaker, Charlie and Maria. The detective preferred to be tended by Maria because she constantly flirted with him. And even though Seff knew Maria only flirted to obtain larger tips, he didn't care, since she was the closest thing to a girl companion in his life. Unfortunately, for the detective, Charlie was the only one bartending tonight.

"Hey, Charlie," Seff said, greeting the bartender.

"It was getting late. I was wondering if you were coming in tonight," Charlie replied.

"Work kept me a little later than usual," the detective responded and paused for a brief second to look around the place. "I don't see Maria, she stand you up tonight?"

"Yeah, she called in sick, left me here all alone tonight."

"You and I both, pal," Seff responded.

"Are you feeling hungry tonight, or are you just here for a drink?" Charlie asked.

"I'm not too hungry, so let me just get a glass of any beer on tap and a shot of bourbon."

"Coming right up."

While Charlie was getting the drink order, Seff lit a cigarette and acknowledged all the other regular customers he recognised. The regulars never spoke in depth, but they would always make small conversations with each other because they were the only friends each one of them had. Charlie soon came back over with the detective's order and placed it in front of him. David wasted no time and swallowed the shot of bourbon, and chased it with the glass of beer. Soon after, the detective ordered another round for himself.

After several glasses of alcohol, Seff typically loosened up and became more sociable, even to unfamiliar people. Strangers generally conversed with the detective for a tiny bit, and then brushed him off as a foreigner in their lives. However, tonight, a woman looking for a conversation and some company sat down next to him.

"Can I get you something to drink, miss?" Charlie the bartender inquired, as soon as the woman sat down. The woman was average height, had a curvaceous figure, smooth skin, curly blonde hair, blue eyes, and she was wearing a dress that showed off her flawless legs.

"I'd like an apple martini, please," the woman replied.

"You got it," Charlie responded.

"I'm just having the worst night," the woman declared. *Whom was she talking to?* The detective wondered. *She didn't walk in with anyone, no one was sitting to the right of her, and the bartender momentarily left to get the drink she ordered. Could it be she was talking to me, the detective contemplated?* Just seconds later, the woman placed a cigarette in her mouth and attempted to light it, but her lighter was broken and only made sparks.

"Here, let me get that for you," the detective insisted, and pulled out his lighter, lighting her cigarette.

"Oh, thank you. That was very kind of you. Just nothing seems to be going right for me tonight. But I'm sure you don't want to hear about it," the woman stated and subsequently chuckled.

"No, on the contrary, I'm very interested," David responded, sounding concerned.

"Here you go, miss, one apple martini," the bartender interrupted.

"Charlie, will you please put the drink on my tab," the detective insisted.

"Not a problem, sir," Charlie replied.

"Believe me when I tell you that I wish my date tonight was as nice as you," the woman declared.

"Well, we are a dying breed," Seff cleverly replied.

"You're telling me! Tonight was my first date in over five years. I remember when guys treated a woman like a lady, not a piece of meat."

"Five years, wow, that's a long time." The detective paused for a brief moment trying to reflect upon the last time he had the company of a woman. It was so long ago, he couldn't recall any. "If you don't mind me asking, why five years? That's such a long time for someone as pretty as you."

"I don't mind," the woman replied and paused for a moment to gather her thoughts. "To make a long story short, it's my daughter's first sleepover party and my first night alone in a long time. I was so hoping to have a nice evening

78

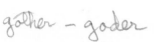
gather — goder

with an adult for a change. Instead, I got stuck with a chauvinistic pig who acted younger than my daughter."

"I'm sorry to hear about your date. The guy sounds like a real jerk." — *estupido*

"Believe me, he was. I couldn't even eat my dinner, he disgusted me so much."

"Well, if you're hungry, I haven't eaten either, and I was just about to sit down and order some food at one of the empty tables. Do you want to join me?" Detective Seff asked.

"I would love to, however, I think I should know your name first," the woman responded.

"My name is David and yours?"

"Paula Dean."

"Well, it's nice to meet you, Paula."

"It's nice to meet you, too, David."

Detective Seff and Paula Dean sat at one of the empty tables and ordered dinner. Their conversation never came to any awkward moments, and never came to an end. After dinner, they decided to continue their conversation inside the warmth of David's apartment. Only minutes after entering the detective's apartment, David and Paula began to kiss.

The kissing started in the living room, but eventually made its way into the bedroom. David didn't bother putting on the lights. He felt it would be more romantic to leave the window shades half-open and let the moonlight dim the room just right. The detective and Paula stopped kissing for a brief moment so he could take off his shoulder holster and lock away his gun. David kept a lockbox in his bedroom where he typically kept his gun when he was off duty. In the meantime, Paula started taking off her cardigan.

Soon after, Paula gently threw the detective flat on his back, but comfortably on the mattress. She then straddled on top of him and unbuttoned his shirt, kissing his bare chest. Paula continued to work her way down, gently kissing him. She stopped just beneath his bellybutton, and unbuckled his belt, unbuttoned his pants, and pulled his slacks and underwear all the way to his ankles. Paula then stood up over

cardigan - troje vestido

awkward - absurda bellybutton - ombligo
aguds

the detective and took off her dress while staring into his eyes. Subsequently, David reached up and slowly pulled down her undergarments.

Paula then gently dropped to her knees squatting over the detective, and their naked bodies touched for the first time. Paula leaned down and slid her legs backward so she was lying on top of him. As soon as Paula's lips came close enough to reach, the detective leaned in and enthusiastically kissed her. In the midst of their kissing and their bodies rubbing against one another, David was falling head over heels for her. He liked the way she kissed and the way she moved her body.

Suddenly, a sound echoed from the shadows of the room immediately causing both the detective and Paula to be still. The noise was a familiar sound that the detective recognised instantly. It was the sound of a gun being cocked. David and Paula quickly looked intensely into the dark corner of the room where they heard the sound. In the shadows stood the frame of a man pointing a gun at the both of them. The detective's first thought was to swiftly grab his gun, but he remembered he locked it up in his safe box. Instead, David immediately pulled Paula behind him, placing a barrier between her and the masked man holding a gun.

"What do you want?" the detective asked nervously for both Paula and himself.

From the shadows of the darkness came a voice. "You're a brave man, Detective, but you should know you're protecting the woman that helped set you up."

"You never said anything about a gun," Paula exclaimed, as she pushed the detective off her and made her way off the bed, scrambling for her clothes. Paula's sudden actions stunned David and left him motionless, used, and silent.

"Relax, you'll get your money," said the voice. "But before you get dressed, I need you to do just one more thing for me."

"I think I've done enough!" Paula barked.

"True, but this will only take a second. Then I won't ask you for anything else but to keep quiet and forget this night ever happened."

"What is it you want me to do?" Paula asked agitatedly.

"There are handcuffs behind you on top of the night table. Take them and bind the detective's hands to the bedpost for me."

"Fine, then I want my money and I'm leaving," Paula stated. She then turned around, walked over to the night table, and picked up the handcuffs.

With the gun still pointed at the detective, the intruder instructed David to place each of his arms on opposite sides of the bedpost behind him. The detective was hesitant at first, but he knew he had no chance to escape. He slowly lifted his arms and placed them where the voice instructed him. "Now Paula is going to strap the handcuffs around your wrists and you're going to stay completely still, and completely quiet. If you try anything funny, you're going to be found bleeding tears from your eyes, and a hole through your heart. Now nod your head if you understand."

Seff knew exactly whom he was dealing with by that statement: the very person he'd been trying to hunt. The detective was scared because he knew the intruder was a person who didn't fear pulling the trigger. With no means of escape, Detective Seff nodded his head and decided to be compliant. Paula walked over to David and placed the handcuffs securely around his wrists, trapping the detective to the bedpost.

The person hiding in the darkness threw an envelope on the floor by Paula's feet. "Inside the envelope you'll find the money I owe you; nothing less, nothing more. Count it if you like." Paula quickly opened the envelope and pulled out a stack of hundred dollar bills. She quickly counted the money, got dressed, and left the apartment.

Shortly after Paula left the bedroom, the man moved from behind the shadows and walked over to the detective with his gun leading the way. The intruder was wearing all black clothing and a mask to hide his face. The only part of the body Seff could see was the intruder's eyes. He thought they were cold, insensible, and didn't show a hint of worry.

When the intruder was a foot away from the detective, he placed the gun only millimetres from Seff's right eye. The detective immediately clenched his eyes shut, held his breath, and let out a little groan, preparing for the worst. Although ALLOW instead of shooting David in the eye, the intruder placed a piece of duct tape over the detective's mouth. When the intruder pulled his gun back, the detective let out a sigh of relief, breathing heavily through his nose.

"I assume I need no introduction," the intruder started to say. "I heard your name mentioned on the news today when some reporter announced that you were leading the investigation of the death of Father Michael. When I heard the news, I just had to meet the person in charge of seeking me out. I know you think I'm crazy, but my victims got what they deserved. They were really victims of their own self-indulgences. I want..." The intruder's voice suddenly trailed away.

A throbbing pain abruptly erupted inside his head, which caused the intruder to immediately rub both his temples with the palms of his hands. The unwelcome guest swiftly took out a bottle of pills from his pocket, and subsequently swallowed a couple. "The voices never quiet down or leave me alone. And as time goes on, they only get louder and louder. I have to hear and see such awful things all the time. Even in my sleep I hear them talking. I didn't ask for this you know, I was chosen. I'm just following the path of my destiny." The intruder suddenly paused and stared intensely at the detective for a brief second.

"By your frightened look I think you have me all wrong. I'm not here to hurt you. I'm here to help you understand and to save you from your impending death. You need to understand my purpose in life has far greater value than your existence. Therefore, if we come face to face again, and you try and stop me, I will not hesitate to take your life or anything else in my path. My advice to you is to drop your current investigation or find another occupation." The trespasser once again paused and took a deep breath before speaking.

"It's not that I don't trust a prostitute, but I shouldn't stay very long. However, before I go, you should know that you and I are very similar. You take down bad people; I do the same, only I do it a little differently. Just understand we're working on the same side, you and me. The people that I have killed are not the pleasant people they seem to be. They're devils disguised as saints, but they were only fooling themselves. I saw who they really were and they had to die.

"Now I hope this will be the last time we meet."

Suddenly, the intruder moved closer to the detective, and raised his gun high into the air. And when the intruder was close enough, he swung the gun downward hitting the back of the detective's head. The striking blow brought David a great deal of pain; however, it did not knock him unconscious. So the intruder hit the detective once again, instantaneously knocking him out cold and bleeding on the back of his head. Then the invader vanished. — desapareció

worst — peor (s) lo peor
GROAM — gemido, lloriqueo
Ailif.
RELIEF — alivio
Throbbing — palpitante, fuerte
Trabéng marcado, estremecí

deserved — merecido
trespasser ↔ violar
Fooling — engaño

Chapter 15

"This is the emergency help line, how may I help you?"

"This is Detective Jacobs, I have an officer down! I need an ambulance right away," he said breathless, nervous to find his partner shackled naked on a bed unconscious, with blood dripping from the back of his head, down his neck toward his lower torso.

"What is your location, sir?"

"Location, Fourteen Mace Way, hurry," Jacobs shouted.

"An ambulance is being dispatched as we speak. They're not far from your location and should arrive any minute," the emergency operator responded. "Can you tell me the officer's name and the details of his present condition?"

"His name is David Seff, he's unconscious, but he has a pulse and he's breathing. He has a deep gash on the back of his head and a little swelling as well."

"Okay, I'm going to relinquish the information to the paramedics en route. In the meantime, if the cut is still bleeding, it would be best if you keep a cloth on it until the emergency unit arrives. Good luck to you, sir, and I hope everything turns out all right," the operator said bluntly, and then disconnected communications with the detective.

"Dave, wake up," Jacobs repeatedly yelled while he grabbed his handcuff key from his pocket. Seff slowly started to regain consciousness as Jacobs released him from his own bracelets.

As soon as Seff became unshackled, he immediately fell to his side. Half-conscious, the detective tried to put together a sentence, but couldn't formulate anything but complete gibberish. "Save your strength, I called an ambulance and they're on their way," Jacobs remarked. The faint sound of sirens became blaring in only a short span of time. An emergency medical team raced up to the detective's apartment and swiftly threw him on a stretcher, however, not before Jacobs was able to wrap a sheet around his unclothed partner. The paramedics then carried the detective down to the ambulance. Jacobs followed shortly behind after he grabbed some of his partner's belongings.

While racing to the hospital, Jacobs called Captain Baron to update him on David's current situation. "Sir, I did just like you asked. I drove over to Detective Seff's apartment, and when I arrived, his door was slightly opened. I went inside and found him handcuffed to his bedpost, lying unconscious with a nasty gash on the back of his head. I immediately called for medical assistance. He's being transported to the hospital in an ambulance as we speak."

"Is he all right?" the captain asked.

"I'm not sure. He was barely conscious when the paramedics took him away. He tried uttering something, but I couldn't make it out. I'm following the ambulance to the hospital; hopefully he'll be more coherent by the time he arrives there."

"All right, I'm leaving the station now, and I'll meet you at the hospital. If anything comes to light before then, call my cell phone."

"Understood, sir," Jacobs replied, then hung up his cell phone.

Detective Seff entered the Abington Memorial Hospital emergency room thirteen minutes after leaving his apartment. One of the staff medical doctors immediately examined him. The cut on the detective's head wasn't significantly deep, but because of the location of the gash, he needed further examination as to any internal damage. To play it safe, the doctor gave the detective a sedative to keep him completely still and free of pain. After several medical examinations, the doctor determined that he was in good health, and subsequently stitched up his wound. Once the detective's head was bandaged, he was given a hospital bed to rest until he regained consciousness from the sedatives.

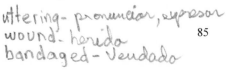
uttering- pronunciar, expresar
wound- herida
bandaged- Vendado

woozy mareado, confuso

When the sleep inducing drug wore off, Detective Seff awoke surrounded by Captain Baron, Detectives Jacobs, Ronald, and Russ. "Good to see you're alive," Captain Baron said.

"It's good to be alive," Seff softly muttered.

"Well, thank your partner; he's the one that found you and called the ambulance." Detective Seff immediately turned to his partner and gratefully thanked him for coming to his rescue.

"Do you know who did this to you?" the captain asked. As woozy as the detective was, he remembered last night's events vividly. It took some time, but David told the group about every detail of last night's escapade.

"Are you sure it was Kevin Mason who did this to you?" Jacobs inquired.

"Well, it was dark and he was wearing a mask, so I can't be certain. It was just the things that he said though, about the voices in his head. It corresponds with the statements he made thirty years ago when he was facing murder charges then, and what his sister told us yesterday. We need to find the girl he hired to set me up last night. If she could identify him and link him to last night's con, then we can link him to the murders. She's our best lead right now." *líder*

"It's more like our only lead," the captain uttered.

"She said her name was Paula Dean, but I doubt that's her real name."

"Jacobs, call Terry; tell her to search our database for anyone named Paula Dean or anyone who's ever used that name as an alias," Captain Baron demanded. "Ronald, Russ, I want you two to take a ride to The Rum Shaker; get a list of names and addresses of whoever was on staff last night. See if any of them know who our mystery whore is. Seff, I know you need some rest, but I need you to come back to the station and look through our face books and the central processing unit for a picture of this woman. Who knows, maybe we'll get lucky. If nothing does come up, I'll need you to sit down with a sketch artist. We need to find this woman immediately."

David Seff was a devoted police officer and a person you could count on. He wasn't going to let a headache stop him from working today. "Sure thing, Captain," the detective replied.

utter - pronunciar, expresar

Chapter 16

Detective Garder was unable to ascertain any information pertaining to Paula Dean or anyone using that name as an alias. Jacobs searched Kevin Mason's bank records and couldn't find any recent large sum withdrawals. Yet after contacting his foster sister, he discovered Mason kept a large safety net of cash in his bedroom she couldn't find. Jacobs also decided to call his paid informants to gather any relevant information about last night's events; however, they knew nothing that could help. Seff looked through mug shots on the computer mainframe for anyone resembling Paula Dean, but was also having no luck. However, in the midst of their unsuccessfulness, Seff and Jacobs were called into the captain's office to find out that Ronald and Russ were able to obtain a picture of Paula Dean.

"The Rum Shaker recently installed several video cameras around their establishment for added security against recent neighbourhood burglaries. They viewed the security tapes and they were able to print a picture of the little slut that set you up last night. They're faxing the picture to my office right now. When it arrives, I want you to run it through the computer and see if we get any positive matches. And gentlemen, if you do get a match, I don't need to tell you two what to do."

"No, sir, you don't," Detective Seff replied. Four minutes later, the fax came though and the detectives gave it to Terry who immediately ran the image through the mainframe for possible matches. The computerised data system was compiled with an abundance of information, and it could possibly take the computer days for it to come up with a match if there even was one to begin with. Luckily, the central processing unit retrieved a mug shot resembling the woman that introduced herself as Paula Dean within the first

match = encuentro
① Una ficha policial parecido

hour. Terry immediately printed out a copy of the mug shot and brought it over to Seff and Jacobs.

"That's her, that's the woman who did this to me!" Seff announced.

"Her real name is Wanda Slone," Garder stated. "She was picked up four months ago for soliciting an undercover cop for sexual services. However, she only spent one night in lock up, and then they let her go. She listed a home address, but it's probably false. I'll go and check to make sure."

"If it's any consolation, she's a lot cuter than I thought she would be," Jacobs commented, trying to be amusing. (A mi sí)

"Thanks, I feel a lot better now," Seff replied. "Make several copies of her mug shot while I touch base with Terry. Be ready to leave in five minutes."

Jacobs nodded and took the picture from Seff's hands. While Detective Jacobs waited for the photocopier machine to free up, Seff walked over to Terry and found out the address Wanda listed was actually a rundown motel.

"Listen," Seff said to Terry. "Both Ronald and Russ are on their way here. As soon as they arrive, give them a picture of Wanda and instruct them to go to the motel. Tell them to ask anyone who works there if they know who she is, but more importantly, if they know where we can find her. If they come up with nothing, have them roam the area with the mug shot. Maybe someone will recognise her. Jacobs and I are taking a drive to where she was picked up for solicitation. Maybe someone there knows who she is."

"I'll let them know," Garder commented.

By the time Detectives Seff and Jacobs drove to Wanda's last known location, the day became night. During daylight hours, this area was typically deserted, however, by night it was just the opposite. At sunset, the site becomes a known area for drug slinging and prostitution. Girls are usually spaced out ten feet apart from one another wearing next to nothing. The good thing about prostitutes is that they run in crews, and if someone isn't part of their crew, they have no problem snitching on them for half their hourly rate.

mug-shot - ficha policial   amusing - chistoso, divertido, gracioso

sunset - puesta del sol, atardecer   site - sitio

It's actually a simple business tactic prostitutes use to eliminate competition.

At this time in the evening, prostitutes and drug dealers come out of hiding and start walking the streets for money. In just a couple of blocks, you can get any type of girl you want. Asian, White, African-American, Indian, Spanish, you name it; you can find it walking in knee high boots, a short dress, see through top, and no undergarments. Detectives Seff and Jacobs inconspicuously drove around the area, calling different women over to their car, flashing Wanda's picture, and asking for information. The girls that didn't blow off the detectives didn't recognise the woman in the mug shot, or at least pretended not to know who she was.

Just as the detectives were willing to concede that what they were doing was a waste of time, a girl by the street name Cherry recognised Wanda's face. Cherry was willing to talk, but the detectives had to pay her sixty dollars for the information. "I haven't seen her around here in a long time, but I know she runs with a pimp named Tahleek Jackson."

"Do you know where we could find this Tahleek Jackson?" Seff asked.

"He hangs out in front of the twenty-four hour liquor store on Bell Avenue. You'll find him there."

A pimp's local hangout spot was more like a business address, and pimps work around the clock. The liquor store wasn't far from the detectives' present location and they were able to drive there in a short time. Tahleek was a small time thug who dabbled in drugs and women. The detectives didn't know what Tahleek looked like, but there was a gentlemen standing in front of the store dressed like a thug dipped in fur. The detectives approached this man believing it was Tahleek. As soon as the guy made eyes on Detective Seff, he immediately ran in the opposite direction. "Tahleek, freeze," Jacobs yelled, but the man just kept running.

Both detectives ran closely behind and chased him for six whole blocks. The pursuit ended when Detective Jacobs tackled Tahleek to the ground and handcuffed, his arms

lobbed - votar

behind his back. Seff stood close behind Tahleek, pointing his gun against the runner's head.

"What's your name?" Jacobs shouted in the individual's ear.

"Get off me, I'm not telling you, jack," the person angrily responded.

→ billetera

"Check to see if he's carrying a wallet," Seff suggested. Jacobs moved aside the uncooperative man's long fur coat, and reached into his back pocket. There he found a black leather wallet and lobbed it over to his partner's free hand. After Seff opened the wallet, he discovered a license that read Tahleek Jackson.

After the detectives confirmed it was the person they were looking for, Jacobs stood Tahleek on his feet. "You know who I am?" Detective Seff questioned, but Tahleek stood silent. "You must know, why else would you run before we even had a chance to introduce ourselves? You should know that running from the police is equivalent to admitting you're guilty."

"I'm not saying shit until I talk to my lawyer, cop," Tahleek shouted. Detective Seff giggled to himself for a moment and then grabbed Tahleek by the collar of his shirt. "Get off me, pig," Tahleek responded. The detective threw him against the building adjacent to where they were standing.

"A man comes into my apartment, ties me up, and assaults me. Soon after, I find out you helped by pimping out one of your whores to help him set me up. Now I ask you, do you really think I'm going to take you to the police station so you can lawyer up and plea bargain your way out of this? Because, if that's what you think, then you're in for a surprise." Then Detective Seff elbowed Tahleek across the face, causing him to fall to the hard pavement, Jacobs decided it would be best for him to turn his back and face the opposite way.

"I don't think you know who you're messing with!" Tahleek yelled.

GRABBED - agarrar 91 coger

"And I don't think you're appreciating your current situation," Seff retorted, as he stuck his knee into Tahleek's chest. The crushing feeling of the detective's knee caused Tahleek to belt out a harsh scream, so the detective covered his mouth with his hand to stifle the screech. "I see you're wearing two hoop earrings in your left ear. I have to tell you, I always wanted an earring. However, I was afraid in my line of work I would get into a scuffle, and some lowlife punk like yourself might purposely rip it out." Seff then grabbed onto one of the hoop earrings and started to tug on it slowly. Staring Tahleek directly in his eyes, Seff yanked the earring out of his ear, slicing Tahleek's earlobe into two parts.

Tahleek let out an awful high-pitched cry, which was muffled by the detective's hand. His earlobe instantly started to bleed. When Seff grabbed the other earring hanging from Tahleek's ear, he started to breathe heavily and begged Detective Seff to stop. "If you want me to stop, start explaining how you know who I am."

"Okay, all right, I'll tell you," Tahleek said and the detective let up a little allowing him to catch his breath. "Yesterday afternoon, one of my girls came up to me and said she was offered five thousand dollars to do this job. The man even gave her five hundred up front, and told her she could have the rest when the job was done. So I ask her, well, what's the job? She said to just follow some guy home from work, seduce him in his own apartment, and make sure the front door is unlocked from the inside."

"Your girl, what was her real name?" Seff asked.

"Wanda, Wanda Slone."

"Go on, I'm listening."

"The guy gave her a picture of a man who turned out to be you with your work address on the back. So later that night, I drove Wanda to the address only to find out it was a police station."

"You knew I was a cop and you still went through with it?" Detective Seff aggressively asked.

"At first I didn't like the idea, but five thousand dollars is a lot of money. And besides, some of my best clients are cops so we waited about four hours until you finally showed your face. From there we followed you to some bar, and that's when Wanda walked into your life. I bet you fell in love with her didn't you?" Tahleek started to laugh. "She has that effect on people. Anyway, after she entered the bar, I drove back here to take care of some business. Wanda was supposed to call me when the job was finished, but she never called. I thought she got busted and gave me up, that's why I ran when I saw you."

"So you're telling me you haven't seen Wanda since last night when you dropped her off?"

"That's right."

"And why should I believe you?"

"Hey, the bitch owes me forty-five hundred dollars from last night's trick. If you think you're the only one looking for her, think again." Tahleek was as low as they come. He only cared about two things, himself and money. While the detective continued to question Tahleek about last night's events, Jacobs received a call on his cell phone from Captain Baron.

"Jacobs, where in the hell is Detective Seff? I've been trying to call his cell phone for the past five minutes and he's not picking up!" the captain said furiously.

"He's been a little busy interrogating a possible suspect from last night's events, sir."

"Well, you tell him to have the suspect transported back here because there's been another murder. And I want you two at the crime scene immediately. Is that understood?"

"Yes, sir, I'll tell him right away."

"Report to sixteen Station Street, and I mean now!"

Chapter 17

The Death of Mark Keller

In the eyes of the innocent, the undeserving receives no compassion and absolutely no forgiveness. The condemned have no conscience, and cannot see right from wrong, but they still carry a soul inside them. When lines are crossed, the unworthy must lose ownership of their essence, so they can burn in the ashes they left behind. As for their future, it becomes unpredictable and unknown, for what lies ahead of them is anyone's guess.

Mark Keller was home alone, or so he thought, making a midnight snack in his kitchen. He left the television blasting from his upstairs bedroom awaiting his return. His wife was away visiting their daughter, so he had the run of the house. After Mark finished concocting a roast beef sandwich, he poured himself a drink and sat down at his kitchen table. As he was about to enjoy the first bite of his snack, the stereo located in the living room abruptly turned itself on stridently, giving Mark quite a scare.

Mark immediately put the sandwich down on his plate, and stood up from the chair. He quickly walked over to the living room so he could figure out what was going on. However, the living room was completely dark and the light switch was on the opposite side of the room. Even when Mark's eyes adjusted to the darkness, it was still hard for him to see the familiar edges of the furniture. The only thing he was able to perceive was the time flashing on the face of the stereo, which didn't help at all. Over the years, Mark has walked through and around the living room many times, where the positioning of the furniture and the space in between was blueprinted in the back of his mind. Thus, Mark felt he would be able to turn off the stereo without the need of light.

Mark led with his hands moving slowly in the direction of the stereo. He felt for familiar landmarks like his leather sofa and the coffee table situated nearby. Mark managed to walk in reaching distance of the stereo system without bumping into one thing. After turning off the music, he slowly began walking back to the kitchen so he could finish his sandwich and go to bed. As he walked back through the darkness, the eyes of the stranger were watching from a close distance.

Mark was easily able to walk back into the kitchen without a problem. Yet he became startled when he noticed his sandwich was missing from his plate. Immediately, Mark looked around confused and scared, then nonchalantly walked to the kitchen telephone to dial the community's private security patrol. However, the phone was dead and Mark realised this might be the beginning of an unpleasant occasion. Though, Mark did have hope. In the house, an emergency button transmits a silent alarm to the security office. Only in order to get to the button, Mark would have to walk through the unlit living room once again.

Mark also had another choice. He could exit the house through the sliding doors in the kitchen and make a run for it. This is what he decided to do. So quickly, Mark ran over to the door and unlocked it swiftly, but by the time he pulled the door open, it was too late. The stranger sent a jolt of electrical current through Mark's body with an electric shock baton. This caused him to fall instantly to the ground. Once Mark hit the floor, the stranger shocked him again for about eight seconds longer, making him weak and disoriented. The stranger then dragged Mark into the living room and threw him down a flight of stairs onto the basement floor.

The fall knocked Mark unconscious, but not for very long. When Mark came to, he probably wished he were already dead. He remembered being pushed into the basement, but Mark couldn't recall how he wound up in the garage, firmly tied to a chair, with a piece of tape across his mouth. His wrists and ankles along with his upper torso were tightly duct taped to the chair, making it hard to move or escape. Mark's eyes were open, not only staring death in the face, but the stranger's as well. He tried to scream something, but the tape over his mouth only muffled his voice.

"I know you're screaming on the inside, but I don't hear a word you're saying," the unwelcome guest uttered. "It's funny how the world works. How everything seems to come full circle. You should have known someone was watching. Someone is always watching. I know you're probably wondering who I am, and how I got here. Some would call it fate, but I would call it your fault.

"So this is where you did it, inside the four walls of your garage. They were screaming too, like the way you're doing now. No one ever heard their cries or their yelling, just as no one is going to hear yours either. The saddest part about their deaths was that even though your victims knew they couldn't be heard, they still tried to scream over and over again. The sound of their own voices echoing in their heads must have been deafening to them. You were the only one that could have stopped it, but you chose to follow through with your desires. Now here I am, roles being reversed, the only one that could stop your death. And though it is not my desire to kill you, I will do it anyway. Know that today isn't about vengeance or revenge, it's about closure."

Mark Keller began to scream frantically, as he tried so hard to wiggle himself free from the tape. Tears fell from the feeling of no hope as the smell of excrement rose from his pants. Mark's face turned bright red from exhaustion and his heavy breathing became the loudest thing in the room. In his mind, Mark was begging the stranger to let him go and be on his way, but the stranger had different plans.

"Mark, I'm going to let you in on what I'm thinking right now because I'm not quite sure what I want to do exactly. Let me rephrase, I know what I want to do, I just don't know which way I'm going to do it yet. You see, I found this old rusted saw with a really dull blade behind your tool cabinet. I don't know, it must have fallen behind the darn thing and was easily forgotten," the stranger articulated, as he flashed the saw back and forth in front of Mark's face. Mark's eyes immediately widened, and lit up out of fear. "I'm just not sure if I should cut your arms and your legs from your torso while you're still alive and breathing, or dead.

"If I choose to do it while you're still alive, I'll make sure you're awake for every second of it. I wouldn't want you to miss the valuable lesson to be learned. Who knows, maybe it will save you somehow when you reach the other side. Then again, I'd be lying if I said I knew anything about where you'd be going. You just better hope it doesn't exist because you're going to burn in the flames of hell if it does. Maybe I'll see you there, but I believe I won't, for this is the last time we will ever meet again.

"Sometimes the hunters become the hunted, and the strong become the weak. The powerful become vulnerable and the helpless gain their peace. The dominant depend on their enemy, but their adversary reveals their true nature, and fatality becomes their conclusion. Pain turns into pleasure, and an awaiting vengeance becomes complete. The cries of sinful temptation are no more, and the presence of an imaginary smile emerges long overdue."

Chapter 18

Once a squad car came to transport Tahleek Jackson to police headquarters, Detectives Seff and Jacobs proceeded to the third crime scene. Ever since they left the hospital, Seff noticed that his partner had been acting a little strange. His concentration seemed to be elsewhere, when it should be focused on the case at hand. This behavior could be a dangerous problem for Detective Seff because in law enforcement, the partner of an unvigilant police officer is typically one that doesn't punch out at the end of the day.

"You okay, Mitch? You look a little out of it. Not to mention you've been acting odd since this morning. Is everything all right?" Seff asked.

"I don't know. I've just been thinking a lot," Jacobs answered.

"Well, what have you been thinking about?"

"Whether or not I'm in the right profession. Our job is to deal with the scum of the earth, where human decency doesn't exist. I know I can die on any given day, but being a police officer just increases the chances. I have a wife and kid to think about. I don't want my daughter growing up without a father, and I don't want my wife to know what it's like to be without me.

"This morning when I saw you tied to your bedpost, bleeding from your head, I thought you were dead. It made me think of my own life. I want to grow old with my wife, and I want to see my daughter become a grown woman."

"Maybe you can put in a request for a desk job or something; you know a position with less worry. Therefore you don't have to lose your pension."

"I don't know. I'm thinking about going back to school, maybe becoming a lawyer or something."

"Yeah, but you're always saying that you hate lawyers."

"It's true I do, but my wife seems to like the idea. Anyway, it was just a thought."

"Well, it's a good thought. I think you'd be an excellent attorney. Mitchell Jacobs Esquire, it's got a nice ring to it."

"Yeah, yeah anyway, did you think Thaleek Jackson was telling the truth? I mean he is Wanda's pimp, he could be trying to protect her."

"To tell you the truth, I don't know. Five thousand dollars is a lot of money; enough money to try and start a new life and leave the prostitution business for good."

"Maybe when we get back to the station, we should ask the captain to put Wanda's face on the front page of a newspaper. Find her that way."

"We could try and hopefully get better results than we're getting with Kevin Mason."

When the detectives arrived at the crime scene, they were immediately greeted by Detectives Ronald and Russ who arrived twenty minutes earlier. Their prior assignment to locate Wanda Slone was a complete failure. No one who worked at the motel knew who Wanda was, and neither did anyone they asked around the surrounding neighbourhood.

After they greeted each other, all four of the detectives made their way over to the dead body. The victim was lying on his back with slight bruising on his face. By the bruising, the disarray of the living room furniture, and broken glass everywhere, it was obvious that there was a scuffle. Russ informed Seff and Jacobs that the victim's name was Andrew McMay.

"The victim was found by his son William, and a group of his friends. They had just gotten back from a four-day camping trip. They found him in the living room, stark nude, shot in both eyes, and in his chest just like the other victims," Ronald said.

"Any witnesses?" Jacobs inquired.

"No, but we spoke to his next-door neighbour and he said that he heard three loud bangs between one and two this morning. He remembered the time vividly because the noise interrupted him during his favourite late night television show," Russ replied.

"The neighbour hears three loud bangs and does nothing but continue to watch his late night television. Sounds like a real good samaritan," Jacobs commented.

"Well, in the neighbour's defence, he did say he walked over to his bedroom window to look outside, but didn't see anything. Then he went back to watching his television programme," Russ retorted.

"So, logic is telling us that Mr. McMay was killed between the hours of one and two A.M. However, that would be impossible," Detective Seff exclaimed. "If the person we're looking for was here committing murder, then who was in my apartment pointing a gun at my head around the very same time? Something doesn't make sense."

"It's possible that the victim wasn't killed between those hours," Jacobs mentioned. "We hear loud noises that sound like gunshots all the time, but aren't gunshots. Those three bangs could have been a number of things. Not to mention, the victim was found naked. Need I remind you who else I found naked this morning." Simultaneously, all of the detectives looked over at Detective Seff. "If you ask me, this makes perfect sense. After our killer left your apartment, he came here. He came here and used the same scheme he pulled on you," Jacobs said, looking at his partner. "Wanda Slone, or maybe some other hooker convinced Mr. McMay to take her back here, so she could seduce him until he was bare and defenseless. Then the killer surprised the victim, however, this time the victim decided to fight back. So there was a scuffle in which Mr. McMay lost, and in turn lost his life because of it."

"It's a good theory, and one in which we shouldn't disregard," Detective Seff declared. "But we also shouldn't rule out the assumption that there might be two killers working together, or this was a copycat murder. Think about it, the details of each of the previous murders have been in almost every newspaper in the state. Anyone keeping up with the news would have enough information to imitate the MO of the killer we're looking for."

"I also sense someone might be trying to mimic Kevin Mason," Russ interjected. "Did you see the front door? It's the first sign of forced entry. Also, the first time there's evidence of a struggle. There have never been signs of a struggle before."

"So it could be the first time the victim saw the murderer before the killer could get the jump on him," Jacobs replied.

"I don't think so. The killer goes to great lengths not to be seen by his victims before he surprises them. Trust me there," Detective Seff said. "Someone do me a favour and help me turn the victim on its stomach." Russ immediately bent down and helped turn the victim over. The detective wanted to see if the killer left a symbol on the back of the victim, in which the killer did.

"We never told the press about the markings," Jacobs shared.

"All right, I want to talk to the son of the victim," Detective Seff decided.

"He's in the kitchen with a couple of uniformed officers," Ronald said. "I could go get him for you if you want."

"No, I'll go to him. It'll be better that way, thanks," Seff responded.

As the detective began to walk toward the kitchen, Jacobs followed behind him. However, Seff asked him to stay behind with the other detectives because he felt it might be easier to talk with William one on one. Therefore, Seff walked into the kitchen alone. Inside the kitchen were two uniformed officers, William, and his girlfriend. With William still in tears, the detective kindly asked the officers and his girlfriend to leave, so he could speak to the victim's son alone. The two officers left immediately, but William's girlfriend was hesitant. However, William assured her that he would be okay, so she left.

William was sitting at the kitchen table, so the detective walked over and sat across from him. He was twenty-two and just graduated college. In a calm, subtle voice, Seff started to speak. "My name is Detective Seff and I want you to know that I am extremely sorry about your loss. I know I can't say anything that will bring you comfort at this moment, but I want you to know that I am in charge of finding your father's killer, and I will do whatever is in my power to bring this despicable murderer to justice.

"I think it's obvious that you really loved your father. And I'm sure you would do whatever was possible to help find his killer." Not expecting a response to the rhetorical statement, William nodded in agreement. "To help find your father's killer, I'm going to need to ask you some questions. I realise you're probably not in the mood to answer questions right now, but in my experience of catching murderers, time is of the essence and you might have the information I need to catch the guy who pulled the trigger. So do you think that maybe you can answer some questions for me?"

Through the tears, sadness, and depression, William agreed to answer the detective's questions. "What did your father do for a living?" Detective Seff asked first.

"He was a reporter for the Crown Newspaper."

"How long has he been working for the paper?"

"I guess for the past twelve years or so."

"Do you read a lot of the articles your father wrote?"

"Most of them, but not all."

"Could you think of an article your father might have written that may have angered someone, and therefore, would want some type of retaliation?"

"No, my father mainly wrote articles about insignificant things that happened in the community. Nothing that would drive someone to want him dead."

"Is there a phone number I can reach your mother at?"

"No, she died from Leukemia when I was sixteen."

"Did your father have a girlfriend?"

"I'm not sure exactly. I know he'd been seeing someone for a little while now, but I've never met or seen her. He never spoke about her to me. It seemed as if they wanted to keep their relationship a secret, so I never bothered to inquire."

"So you don't know this woman's name, or know where we could find a picture of her?"

"Sorry."

"Does your father typically keep his girlfriends a secret from you?"

"He tried. I think he thought it would hurt me, you know to see him with someone besides my mother. It was something we just never talked about. It would have been okay though if he met someone else. I would have been okay with it."

"William, can you think of any reason why someone would want to murder your father?"

"No, he was a great man. Never in my life have I ever seen him hurt someone else." William couldn't suppress his sadness anymore and started to burst into tears and cry heavily for his father's death. The detective immediately raised himself out from his chair and grabbed William by his shoulder.

"Listen, your father would be very proud of you right now for being so strong and answering these hard questions. Not many people could have done that. From what I gathered, your father seemed like a great man and his death was undeserving. And like I said before, I will do everything in my power to bring your father's killer to justice." William looked into the determined eyes of Detective Seff and felt a sense of ease, but did not stop tearing. "I'm going to give you my card. It has my work number on the front, and I wrote my cell phone number on the back. If you need anything, and I mean anything at all, please don't hesitate to call. Now, do you have a place to stay for a couple of days besides this house?" William once again nodded his head in the positive. "Good, it will probably be best if you stay there, and besides,

103

we need to close off the property for a couple of days while we sort things out. You're going to be all right, I promise. I'm going to go back in the other room now. I'll send your girlfriend back in."

As Detective Seff was leaving the kitchen, he suddenly stopped before the kitchen door. He turned his head to the left and saw a set of steak knives on the kitchen counter. He noticed that the set of knives were a little dusty except for one that was noticeably clean. The detective instantly walked over to examine the blades. However, before he had a chance to inspect the knives, he came across a tiny smudge of blood directly under the handle of a nearby drawer. The bloodstain was smaller than the tip of a number two pencil, but it was big enough for the detective to catch it.

"Officers," Detective Seff shouted softly. Immediately, the two uniformed officers ran inside the kitchen.

"Yes, sir?" the ranking officer said while the other stayed silent.

"I'm going to need you to take William outside for some fresh air, and on your way out, please ask the crime scene specialist to come see me in here."

"Sure thing, sir," the ranking officer said.

While the officers took William out of the kitchen, Seff opened the kitchen drawer marked with the tiny bloodstain. Inside the drawer were a variety of different sized knives scattered and unorganised. Instinctively, the detective opened the only two other drawers inside the kitchen. The other bins contained silverware and other utensils, only the contents in these drawers were neatly placed in an orderly fashion.

Suddenly, the crime scene specialist appeared. Her name was Stephanie Baptiste. Detective Seff has known Stephanie for about three years. They are frequently in contact with one another, but only because she analyses evidence on many of the detectives' homicide cases. "Detective Seff, how are you?" Stephanie rhetorically asked. "The uniformed officer outside told me that you requested my presence."

DRAWer - Cojon

"Yes, I did. I found a spat of blood on this drawer here," he said, pointing to the stain. "I need you to analyse it along with all the contents inside the drawer."

Curious to see the contents inside of the bin, Stephanie opened it and saw the different assortment of knives. "You think the killer might have used one of these knives on the victim, then cleaned it, and put it back in the drawer?"

"No, I think the killer is smarter than that. However, the killer might have used his fingers to rummage through the knives before he chose the weapon. If you look inside the other kitchen drawers, you'll find them to be exceptionally tidy. Yet, the contents inside the drawer with the bloodstain are all cluttered, and I think the killer made the mess."

"It's a theory with potential, I'll give you that. All right, I'll analyse the bloodstain and check for latent bloodstains and fingerprints on and around the drawer. As for the contents inside the drawer, who knows, maybe we'll get lucky."

"Maybe we will. I'll talk to you soon then. I have to go in the other room and speak with the other detectives."

"I'll call you as soon as I have something."

Before Detective Seff left the kitchen, he took one last look around. He then walked over to the other detectives who were still analysing and debating over whether or not this murder was a copycat of the others. Seff informed the other detectives about the details of the interview, the bloodstain found on the drawer, and the contents it held inside. Then he instructed the detectives to spread out around the house and search for other clues.

rummage — hurgar, escarbar
cluttered — desordenado.
(desler)
bloodstain — manchade sangre

Chapter 19

The Stranger and the Prostitute

Inside a room, there was a closed wooden box, no bigger than an adult-sized coffin. Each panel of wood was six inches thick and extremely durable. Inside the box was extremely hot and uncomfortable with nothing to see but complete darkness. There were cracks allowing fresh air to seep within, but it was still hard for Wanda Slone to breathe. She had woken from a nightmare, dazed, confused, trapped and very scared.

Gasping for air, Wanda opened her eyes only to see darkness. Confused by her surroundings, Wanda felt around with her hands and feet trying to find an opening, or some other means of escape. However, the box was nailed shut from every angle and locked by key on the outside for extra security. Frustrated and scared, Wanda immediately started to kick the wooden panels as hard as her momentum would allow. Although, all she was doing was wasting oxygen and energy.

"Help," Wanda screamed repeatedly, as she hysterically began to cry. Wanda's screams were ineffective, since no one could possibly hear her. It's true, the box wasn't soundproof, but the room in which the box was placed in was. It was false to say that no one could hear Wanda scream. There was one person who was listening, and he was sitting in a chair four feet away from her, staring directly at the box.

Squirming inside the box, Wanda positioned herself so she could look through a tiny crack, which was emitting a minuscule amount of light. However, the crack was too small, and she wasn't able to see anything. Wanda's cries eventually came to a halt and the only thing she was able to hear was her own breathing. Suddenly, a soft squeaking sound disseminated through the air. The sound came from the stranger when he repositioned himself in his chair.

"Who's there, is someone there?" Wanda screamed. "Let me out of here!" she yelled, as she banged on the box's walls with her hands and feet. Wanda's requests were answered by silence, and it took some time until she concluded that the sound wasn't made by a person. It wasn't until later when she heard footsteps pacing around the box that she knew she wasn't alone. "Why are you doing this to me?" Wanda shouted. "Let me out of here," she cried.

For quite a while, the stranger said nothing. All he did was slowly walk around the box collecting his thoughts. In fact, the man said nothing until she gave up yelling and crying for freedom. "Wanda Slone. That is your name isn't it?"

"Who are you? Why are you doing this to me?" Wanda cried.

"I'm here to make things right. You don't know me, but I know you very well. I know all about you and everything you stand for. I probably know you better than you know yourself."

"Let me out of here," Wanda repeated while kicking the box. "Help!" she screamed from the top of her lungs.

"Before you tire yourself out, you should know something. You're in a box in a room that is soundproof. No matter how loud you scream, kick, or yell, no one is going to hear you except me."

"I don't believe you," Wanda replied. "Help!" Wanda shouted.

"Maybe you'll believe this; you're going to die within twenty minutes. As it stands right now, your body is able to receive the air it needs to survive. When our conversation is over, I'm going to wrap the box in plastic, preventing any air from entering. Therefore, the more you breathe, the less time you have to live. Then after you've sucked in your last breath and your body gives into death, I'm going to take out my gun and shoot you three times, but don't worry, you won't feel a thing."

"Please, I've never done anything to you," Wanda screamed. "Let me go, I don't want to die. I'll do anything, just let me go."

"I don't know why you're complaining and begging for your life. Do you really think your life is worth saving? You sleep around with hundreds of men you don't even know for cash. These are men with diseases, men who beat you for fun, and men with wives who have children. When you're not prostituting yourself, you're inserting poison into your arm. Sometimes you use a clean needle and sometimes you use a dirty one.

"The bottom line is you have no respect for yourself and the way I see it, your life is meaningless. It serves no purpose at all, and I feel no pity for someone who doesn't care for themselves. Why live when you're living for no reason except to destroy yourself?"

"I could be a better person. I could change, I swear. Give me another chance," Wanda begged. "Let me go, please, I don't want to die."

"It's too late, and I don't believe you anyway. Your life was headed down this direction way before we ever met. I'm just speeding up the process."

"I don't deserve this. I don't deserve to die like this," Wanda pleaded between cries. "You're going to get yours someday, and I hope you burn in hell!" Wanda shouted.

"That might be true, but unlike you, I don't have to deal with that burden today. You know, this whole time that you've been begging for your life, not once did you mention your baby son, and how you're going to miss him. Or that if you die, there is no one else that will take care of him. A comment like that might have persuaded me to change my mind about ending your life. Has heroin messed your mind up so badly that you don't even remember your own son?"

"How do you know this? Why are you doing this to me?" Wanda said, as she wept. "Take me out of this box."

Wanda screamed and began to kick the box harder than before.

"Do you remember leaving him alone for someone else to find?" The stranger yelled.

"What kind of life could I have given him?" Wanda sobbed. "I can't even take care of myself," she yelled.

"If you didn't want to take care of your child, you could have given the baby to his father."

"How could I do that when I don't even know who the real father is? Or did you forget I'm a prostitute and I've slept with hundreds of men."

"Wanda," the man said, as he moved to sit on top of the box. "We both know exactly who the father of your child is. I even believe he loved you. I could honestly say he would have taken you away from all your problems, given you a life worth living."

"At least two guys a night offer to take me off the street and give me a better life. But they soon forget almost immediately after they cum," Wanda sobbed.

"No, this guy was different, unlike most of your customers. He respected you, bought you food to eat, showed you it was possible to smile again. It's possible that you two could have saved each other."

"You don't understand. I just couldn't leave my employer. There would have been consequences."

"There was no reason stopping you from running far away and starting a new life somewhere else."

"Well, you don't know my pimp very well; he has connections all over the place. He would have found me and then killed me. And after he killed me, he would have killed my son, along with anyone else he thought might have taken me away from him. I was trying to help my baby," Wanda groaned. "I had no means to take care of him. What kind of life could I have given him?" she shrieked.

"I guess you'll never know," the stranger said, as he lifted himself off the box and took hold of an oversized roll of plastic wrap in the corner of the room. "Wanda, we met by chance, but now you'll die by choice." Instantly, Wanda started to kick and scream, even louder and harder than all the previous times before. As the kicking and screaming went on, the stranger wrapped the box in plastic. He made sure all the cracks were covered so no oxygen could find its way inside. After about two minutes, the whole box was sealed in plastic. And not long afterward, the banging inside the box came to a halt, and Wanda's screams ended.

To be safe, the stranger didn't remove the plastic wrapping until two hours after Wanda's kicking and screaming ended. When the box was finally dismantled, Wanda's body was without life. Her skin turned light blue and grey, and three of her nails broke into the top panel of the box from trying to pry it open. There was no doubt Wanda was dead, yet the stranger took out his gun and fired three bullets into her body, just as the stranger said he would do.

Chapter 20

Soon after the detectives finished investigating the crime scene at the home of the deceased, Andrew McMay, Detective Seff decided to call it a night and start fresh in the morning. However, the morning would come quicker than the detective thought. It was 4 A.M. when his telephone rang and woke him from a sound sleep. Barely awake, the detective picked up the telephone on his night table and said, "Hello," in a raspy voice.

"Get dressed; I just got a call from Lieutenant Mosley over at the third precinct. They found your prostitute dead in a dumpster near the loading docks," Captain Baron said, relaying the message. "Get in touch with Detective Jacobs and fill him in. Then tell him to meet you down at the docks at once. Oh, and I expect a full report of the details by the time I get into my office around eight o'clock. Is that understood?"

"Sure thing, Captain," Detective Seff responded, still half-asleep. Subsequently, the detective hung up the phone and jumped out of bed. He quickly threw cold water on his face to wake him up. After that, he called Jacobs and filled him in on the situation. "Yeah, so I'll meet you at the harbour by the loading docks in about twenty-five minutes."

"I'll be there," Jacobs replied.

After Seff got off the telephone, he rapidly washed up, got dressed, and left for the harbour in less than fifteen minutes. The loading docks weren't far from his apartment, and being that there were hardly any other cars on the road at this time, the detective arrived at the docks quickly. The police set up a barricade even though there were no pedestrians in sight. Detective Jacobs arrived at the loading docks only minutes after his partner. The two detectives entered the secured area together.

DUMPSTER - contenedor de basura
PURSE - Bolso

Once inside the barricade, Seff instantly reached into his left hand pocket and grabbed a cigarette out of a pack he found under the seat of his car. He then quickly lit it and vigilantly looked around. There were police officers scattered all over the docks searching and probing around with their flashlights. The positioning of all the police officers and the size of the area made it hard for the detectives to locate where the dead body was situated. Therefore, Detective Seff decided to ask the first officer they passed to point them in the right direction.

"Excuse me, officer, can you tell us where we can find the body that was found in the dumpster?" Seff kindly asked, showing the officer his badge.

"Just go straight ahead and make a right at The Bait and Tackle Store, you can't miss it." The detectives followed the officer's directions and sure enough, Wanda Slone's body was lying on the ground on top of a black body bag. The corpse was being looked over by two forensic crime scene specialists who the detectives didn't recognise. Therefore, instead of making small talk, Detective Seff and Jacobs wasted no time introducing themselves and asked what they could tell them about the dead woman.

"Her name is Wanda Slone or was for that matter. She was found by harbour patrol while they were making their rounds. One of the officers spotted an arm hanging out of this dumpster here," the specialist said, pointing at an old rustic blue waste container. "So they decided to take a closer look and discovered her body. They found her identification in her purse, which was tied around her neck. Whoever killed her did a real number on her. Shot her twice in the face, taking out both eyes, and once in the chest. However, we haven't been able to find any of the bullets or the casings yet. And to be honest, I don't think they're going to be found."

"Oh yeah, and why's that?" Jacobs asked.

"We looked all over this area for bloodstains, observable and latent, but we didn't find any. If the victim was shot at this location, there would be an abundance of evidence of blood splatter, but there isn't."

"So you're saying the body was dumped here without the bullets or the casings?" Detective Seff interjected.

"Exactly," the crime scene specialist replied.

"Was there any money found in the purse?" Seff asked next.

"Besides her identification, a comb, and some prophylactics, there was nothing."

"What about her back?" Jacobs asked. "Did the killer leave some sort of marking?"

"It looks like a small blood splatter right now, but, yeah, it's some kind of marking."

"Good, just make sure the incisions on her back are photographed and placed in the autopsy report. And then have a copy of the report sent to me ASAP," Detective Seff ordered, handing his card to the nearest crime scene specialist.

Twenty minutes later, Wanda's body was bagged for transportation. The two specialists left not too long afterward. Later that same hour, while the detectives were investigating the crime scene, three uniformed police officers came over to the detectives and stood in a triangular formation. "We're looking for Detective Mitchell Jacobs?" the officer who stood in front asked firmly.

"Yes, that would be me," Detective Jacobs declared, stepping in front of the three officers. "What can I do for you, I'm a little busy."

Immediately, two of the officers positioned themselves on opposite sides of Detective Jacobs. "You could make this as easy as possible. We have been given orders to place you under arrest and take you into custody."

"Arrested for what?" Seff asked agitatedly, becoming hostile.

"Mitchell Jacobs, please put your hands on top of your head," the officer standing adjacent to Mitchell demanded, ignoring Detective Seff's question. However, Jacobs didn't comply and kept his hands by his side.

"No one is arresting anybody until I get some answers!" Seff shouted. "Or do I have to remind the three of you who outranks who here?"

"These orders come directly from Captain Baron, who outranks you, sir," the officer stated. "Please take Detective Jacobs into custody." Instantly, the officers standing on the side of the detective took a hold of his wrists and gently pulled them behind his back. Jacobs didn't resist and allowed himself to be handcuffed without difficulty. After Mitchell's wrists were bound together, the officers took his badge and removed his gun from his waist. Then as one of the three officers were reading Jacobs his Miranda Rights, the other officers patted him down in case he was holding additional weapons.

"Mitchell Jacobs, you are under arrest for the murder of Andrew McMay. You have the right to remain silent, anything you say can be held against you in a court of law. You have the right to consult an attorney. If you can't afford an attorney..."

As Mitchell was being read his rights, Detective Seff was trying to reach Captain Baron by telephone so he could get to the bottom of the current situation.

"Captain Baron."

"Captain, this is Detective Seff, what is going on? Why is my partner being arrested for Andrew McMay's murder?"

"Detective, never mind that, your focus should be on catching Kevin Mason and that's it."

"You just can't tell me to never mind that!" the detective said heatedly. "He's been my partner for eight years and I deserve to know what's going on. Not to mention if anyone should have detained Mitchell, it should have been me, or at the very least, conducted in a less humiliating manner."

"Well, your soon-to-be ex-partner dug himself into a grave he's not going to be able to dig himself out of, and I'm afraid neither you nor I can do a goddamn thing about it!"

Captain Baron yelled back. "We'll deal with this matter later. So finish up there, and then report to the station as soon as you're done. We'll discuss it then." The captain subsequently hung up the phone without giving Seff a chance to reply.

Not knowing exactly what to do, Detective Seff watched as his partner was taken away in handcuffs and driven off in the back of a squad car. In the back of his mind, the detective knew Captain Baron wouldn't have Jacobs arrested on a hunch or for some speculative reason. So there must be a good explanation behind his decision. One which Detective Seff was eager to learn.

Chapter 21

One hour later, Detective Seff finished investigating the crime scene. He couldn't find any additional evidence other than Wanda's dead body. Seff knew the autopsy would be done within a couple of hours and the only thing left to do was to wait. Therefore, the detective followed the captain's orders and left the crime scene for the police precinct.

During the ride to the station, thoughts of curiosity ran through the mind of Detective Seff. It wasn't so much of why Kevin Mason murdered the woman who conspired to help set up the detective, but why his partner was ripped from the investigation and arrested for murder. For a police officer to be taken into custody in the midst of trying to catch a notorious serial killer there must be strong evidence against him. But what evidence?

After the detective parked his car and entered the police station, he walked upstairs to his desk. What he really wanted to do was walk inside the captain's office and be informed of his partner's current situation. However, the captain's door was closed and the number one rule of the station is if his door is shut, he is never to be disturbed for anything. Something big must be going on behind that door. The captain even closed the blinds covering the glass windows surrounding his office, which is something he rarely does.

Suddenly, Detective Garder rolled up behind Seff and asked him, "What's going on? First they arrest Mitchell's wife, then Mitchell, and now they're talking to his wife in the captain's office?"

"Who's talking to his wife?"

"The captain, some forensic specialist, and a couple of men from internal affairs."

"How long have they been talking with her?"

"Probably around forty minutes or so."

"Well, to be honest, I don't know what's going on," Seff exclaimed. "Do you know where they're holding Mitchell? I'd like to speak with him."

"He's being held downstairs in holding cell B, but Captain Baron made it specifically clear that nobody is to speak with Mitchell until he says otherwise. If you go down there, you're putting your job and maybe your freedom in jeopardy, and believe me when I say it's not worth it. Whatever's happening to Mitch isn't your doing and it certainly isn't your problem. If he did something wrong, don't let him bring you down with him because of it. You're more intelligent than that."

Just as Terry was finishing lecturing the detective, Stephanie Baptiste, the forensic specialist who conducted the lab testing for Andrew McMay's death, walked out of Captain Baron's office. Seff quickly excused himself and darted over to talk with Stephanie. "Weren't you supposed to call me as soon as you found anything out about Mr. McMay's case?" the detective asked in a not so kind tone.

"Yes, I know, but due to extenuating circumstances, I had no other choice but to follow other procedures first," Stephanie answered.

"Well, you just can't keep me in the dark. My partner was arrested for a crime I'm investigating."

"Well, if it's any consolation, you're no longer investigating Andrew McMay's death," Stephanie assured the detective, as she looked at the time on her watch. "I have to go; I'm running late for another meeting downtown."

"You can't just go without telling me something. Anything," Detective Seff begged.

"Listen, I can't talk here," she whispered, staring at the captain's door. "There are too many eyes and ears around here. If you want to talk, meet me outside behind the post office across the street in three minutes after I leave. If you're late then I'm leaving." Stephanie then nonchalantly walked past Seff and made her exit.

SMIDGEN- pizca, el poquito

Behind the post office, Seff found Stephanie waiting for him, smoking a cigarette. The detective decided to smoke as well, to give the impression of two people having a casual conversation. Stephanie immediately told David she felt very uncomfortable talking with him about his partner's case. "This is off the record because I could lose my job for this," Stephanie uttered. "You understand that, right?"

"Yes, of course," the detective answered. "Off the record."

"The smidgen of blood you found on the drawer in Andrew McMay's kitchen belonged to him. I found small traces of his blood inside the drawer as well, but no evidence of anyone's fingerprints. However, your partner's wife's fingerprints were discovered all over the victim's house. And after confronting her about it, she admitted to having an affair with Andrew McMay, but she claims it was your partner who shot him. He caught the two of them in the midst of a sexual encounter, and didn't hesitate to put three bullets in the victim. During the interrogation, Mrs. Jacobs also asserted that after her husband shot Mr. McMay, he went into the kitchen and came back with a knife, and told her to leave."

"Do you believe her?" Seff asked.

"She told us where we could find the murder weapon and the knife. When we find them, your partner's going down for murder. Now I really am late, and I have to go. Remember, this conversation was off the record."

"You don't have to worry, I won't say a word to anyone," the detective assured Stephanie, as she walked away. Soon after, Seff walked back to his desk at the station contemplating Mitchell's situation and what he could do to help. However, his thoughts went elsewhere after he noticed there was one unheard message on his voicemail. The message was from the medical examiner's office. They called to inform him that Wanda Slone's autopsy was completed, and that he should contact them immediately.

It wasn't long after that the detective was on the telephone with Dr. White, the individual who performed the autopsy. "You, my friend, have a very interesting case on your hands," the doctor mentioned to the detective.

"Yeah, tell me something I don't know," Seff answered.

"Well, to start with, Wanda Slone didn't die from three gunshot wounds. She actually suffocated to death before the killer decided to shoot her."

"Why would anyone suffocate someone and then shoot them? It just doesn't make any logical sense," the detective reasoned.

"Well, it might. During the autopsy, I came across evidence of internal tearing of the fascia muscles of Wanda's pelvic floor, which are often caused by the trauma of extracting a baby's head through the pelvic diaphragm during labour. However, I couldn't find any records of Wanda ever giving birth to a child."

"It's not abnormal," Seff interjected. "You'd be surprised how many women sell their child on the black market. People pay a lot of money for a newborn baby and even more to keep it under wraps. But I don't understand how this is connected with her murder."

"Since there were signs of a pregnancy and no record of it, I followed proper procedures and took a sample of Wanda's DNA. Then I cross-referenced it with all the Jane and John Doe DNA samples we have in our database. The computer came up with a ninety-nine percent match to a deceased baby boy."

"How did the baby die?" the detective asked.

"Well, that's the most interesting part," the doctor exclaimed. "The autopsy report said the baby was found inside a dumpster, within a plastic bag, and died by asphyxiation moments after birth. In other words, the baby died just as his mother did. Not to mention both of their bodies were discovered in a dumpster."

"That is interesting." *It couldn't be just a coincidence that the child and the mother were murdered in the same exact fashion,* the detective thought. "Doctor, does the report give a date of when the child was murdered?"

WRAPS - envolturas   119

"The report stated seven years ago. Listen, I have to perform another autopsy in just a little while. How about I have one of the interns here make a copy of both autopsy reports for you? You can pick them up or I can have them faxed over to you."

"If you can have someone fax the reports as soon as possible, it would be great." The detective responded.

"I'll get someone right on it."

"Thank you for your help," the detective expressed.

"It's my job," the doctor replied.

After the detective hung up the phone, he sat back in his chair and imagined Wanda Slone suffocating her new born baby. The detective began to think Wanda's death felt more like revenge and not so much a random murder. *But how is Kevin Mason connected to Wanda Slone? What if there is no connection? What if Mason really possesses this extraordinary ability? Now I'm starting to sound crazy. But what other lead do we have?*

random murder - asesinato al azar .

Chapter 22

Instead of sitting at his desk, waiting for another murder, Detective Seff decided to revisit St. Paul's Church where the late Father Michael was shot. As the detective was driving, he decided to make a phone call to Detective Russ and instruct him and his partner to revisit the late Mark Keller's home. "Maybe we overlooked something we can't see," Detective Seff said.

"You're the boss," Detective Russ commented.

When Seff arrived at the church, he was greeted by Father Schmitt. Father Schmitt has taken over all responsibilities of the church since Father Michael's passing.

"Father Schmitt, it's nice to see you again," Detective Seff said cordially. "How is everything?"

"As you can probably guess, it's a sad time around here. How is the investigation going?" Father Schmitt asked curiously. "I hope you're making some headway."

"We're making progress but nothing worth bragging about."

"So what can I do for you?" the priest questioned.

"Some new evidence has come to light that might explain the reason behind Father Michael's death, and if you don't mind, I would like to look inside Father Michael's office one more time."

"That shouldn't be a problem." Father Schmitt responded. "I keep the door locked, so you'll have to wait a minute while I get the key."

"Sure," the detective replied. "Oh, before I forget, I also called a K9 unit to meet me here. They haven't arrived yet, but when they do I hope you don't mind if they sniff around. Just in case we might have overlooked something."

"If it will help, it's not a problem."

Father Schmitt left for a brief moment and obtained the key from his office. Upon his return, he opened the office door and let Seff inside. As the detective re-examined the office, Father Schmitt looked on, never leaving him alone for one moment. Detective Seff meticulously went through every file, piece of paper, photograph, and book lying around Father Michael's office, but discovered nothing new. Nothing was arousing the dog's suspicion either.

After an hour, the search was running dry and Detective Seff was about to give up and revisit the priest's home. However, there was a celestial painting of Jesus hanging on the wall that attracted the detective's attention. It wasn't so much the painting itself that intrigued him; it was the size of the portrait and the way it slightly protruded off the wall. Seff walked over to the painting and stared at it for about a minute. He then took his fingers and slowly felt around the frame of the painting, and discovered it was being held up by two hinges, almost invisible to the human eye. The painting was merely a covering for a secret wall safe.

After the detective discovered Father Michael's personal vault, he looked over at Father Schmitt and questioned his knowledge about the hidden safe. However, the priest wouldn't admit to any awareness of the safe or its combination. "Father Michael was a priest here for many years before I was. I'm just as surprised as you are," Father Schmitt said convincingly. "It's something he never revealed to me."

"Well, do you know of anyone who might know the combination? Because I hate to tell you what we might have to do to this wall in order to get this metal box open."

"I'm afraid the only person I know who had knowledge of the combination is no longer among the living," Father Schmitt replied.

"I guess we're at a stalemate aren't we," Seff whispered softly to himself. "I actually might know a guy who could help," the detective uttered, as he took out his cell phone and called Terry back at the station. "Hey, it's Seff. I need you to obtain the phone number of Gabriel Molina. I'm almost positive he's in the mainframe, but you might have to call his parole officer to find out his current phone number."

"I'll get right on it," Detective Garder replied.

"Get back to me soon, thanks."

Gabriel Molina was busted nine years ago for bank robbery. He broke into Dimes Savings Bank without setting off the alarm at night while no one was there. He was also able to bypass eleven motion sensors and fifteen video cameras. But the most impressive thing he did was open a timed lock, ten-inch thick steel plated vault when it was sealed shut and supposedly impenetrable for another eight hours. He was caught six days later when he used several marked bills to purchase a used car.

Gabriel gave back all of the money he didn't spend, the valuables he stole, and served eight years of a ten-year prison sentence. He was let out of prison two years early for good behaviour. As soon as he was released, he was hired as a consultant by the same security company that constructed the vault he cracked eight years earlier. Due to his parole guidelines, Gabriel isn't allowed to leave the state, so he is forced to consult within the boundaries of Pennsylvania.

After Terry retrieved Gabriel's home phone number, she gave it to Detective Seff. The detective called Gabriel several times before he actually picked up the phone. He agreed to help the detective, but only if he was able to convince his parole officer to permit a two-week vacation to California. Immediately, Seff was on the phone with Gabriel's parole officer, trying to persuade him to allow Gabriel to have two weeks in California. His parole officer agreed to one week's vacation in a neighbouring state, but that was it.

Even though Gabriel wasn't ecstatic about visiting any other state besides California, he thought the deal was better than nothing. Therefore, he agreed to help the detective. Gabriel told Seff that he would be at the church within an hour. While waiting for Gabriel, the detective made another phone call, but this time to Detective Russ. "Did you find anything?" Seff asked.

"The dog just got here; let me call you back in a little while," Russ answered back.

"I'll be waiting."

Forty-five minutes later, Gabriel was standing in Father Michael's office holding a bulky brown bag. He immediately stood in front of the wall safe and studied it, but not for very long. Gabriel recognised the make and model of the safe, but couldn't believe someone still used such an antiquated unit. It only took minutes for Gabriel to crack the safe open and live up to his end of the bargain. As soon as the door to the safe was opened, the detective swiftly looked inside.

The safe only contained two objects, a manila folder and a card box. The detective first grabbed the light yellow brown folder and opened it. Inside was the deed to the church and nothing else. Then after placing the folder down on Father Michael's desk, the detective grabbed the card box and wasted no time opening it.

Inside the card box were fifteen photographs of young children. Some of the photographs were of little boys, and some were of young girls. In all the pictures, all the children were fully dressed, except for one. The last photograph Detective Seff turned to was a picture of Father Michael with his shirt off, holding a seven year old boy's genitals. Detective Seff couldn't believe his eyes.

Father Schmitt was also in shock or acted the part very well. The detective left the church with the black box and brought it directly to the crime lab, so the pictures could be analysed for authenticity and fingerprints. Soon after dropping off the pictures at the crime lab, Russ called Detective Seff. "We just dug up a right foot and a left hand with two fingers. But the dogs are running around the entire backyard going absolutely crazy."

"Listen, I want you to deliver that hand to the crime lab ASAP. I'm there now. Have Ronald stay behind and continue to dig. I'll get him more help as quickly as I can."

"I'll let him know and I'll meet you at the crime lab," Russ said too quickly to understand.

While Detective Seff waited for the analysis report and Detective Russ' arrival, he decided to call Captain Baron and update him on the current situation. However, when he called, the detective was only able to reach his voicemail, so he left him a message to call him back whenever possible. Since a lot has been going on in the past couple of hours, Detective Seff unintentionally forgot about his partner's situation. Now that things have slowed down a bit, he began to wonder what was happening to Mitchell. And right in the midst of his curiosity, the captain called him back.

"Detective, it's Captain Baron, sorry I missed your call, but I was just finishing up talking with internal affairs. I want you to know that your partner admitted to murdering Andrew McMay out of a jealous rage. Now I know this news might be hard to take, but you need to remember you're a cop, and you're on a very important case. You need to stay focused on your case and put your partner's situation on the side right now. Do you think you can do that?"

Detective Seff took a brief moment to think about it and answered, "I'll do my best."

"Good, now that we can put that temporarily behind us, what's the latest news on the Mason investigation? I have a meeting with the chief of police and the mayor in an hour, and they want to be updated on the latest events. I hope you have something good for me to tell him."

"Sir, I have news, but I don't think you're going to like it."

"You know my time is short so don't sugarcoat it, just spit it out detective."

"Wanda Slone's autopsy revealed she had given birth, but there was no record of her ever having a baby. To make a long story short, her DNA was matched to a baby boy who was suffocated to death minutes after it was born. This means Wanda more than likely murdered her own child soon after it was born. Since I had no leads to follow, I decided to reinvestigate Father Michael and instructed Detectives Russ and Ronald to do the same for Mark Keller. While investigating the priest, I discovered a hidden wall safe that contained several pictures of young children, and on picture of Father Michael committing a sexual act on a young boy."

"Are you telling me that Father Michael was a child molester?" Captain Baron exclaimed.

"I'm at the crime lab right now waiting for an analysis of the pictures authenticity. But yeah, that's what I'm saying."

Captain Baron sat back in his chair and said, "I can't believe this."

"I'm not finished. Detectives Russ and Ronald discovered a foot and a hand with only two fingers in the backyard of Mark Keller's house. The body parts were found underground near the tree in which his body was discovered. I believe Mr. Keller murdered someone himself, chopped up the body, and buried the parts in his backyard. Russ is on his way here with the body parts, so we can identify who they belonged to."

"Are you telling me that Kevin Mason is murdering criminals?"

"Yeah, that's exactly what I'm saying."

"Well, how does Kevin Mason know about their crimes?" the captain asked.

"I don't know. There aren't any connections between Mason and his victims, and there aren't any connections between the victims themselves. I hate to say it, but maybe Kevin Mason really does have the power to see the evil within people."

"Are you honestly telling me you believe that?"

"To be honest, I don't know what to believe. This is all too surreal."

"Is that what you expect me to go to the mayor with? Our serial killer has psychic powers and only kills people who commit heinous crimes?"

"No, I'd tell him everything I told you, and that we're doing everything we can to find a connection between the victims and the suspect we believe is behind the killings."

"Listen very carefully, Detective. As soon as you find out anything more, I expect to be the first one notified. Is that clear?" the captain demanded.

"Affirmative, sir."

Chapter 23

Four hours had passed since Detective Seff got off the phone with Captain Baron. During that time, Detective Russ delivered the body parts to the Pittsburgh crime lab. His partner delivered sixteen additional human remains from the same backyard. The extremities found belonged to three women who were all homeless and deaf-mute. It just so happens that Mark Keller was volunteering at a clinic for the deaf, so he found victims he could rape and murder that couldn't scream, and wouldn't have anyone come searching for them after they were deceased.

The pictures that were found in Thomas Michael's wall safe were authentic, but unfortunately, there was only one set of fingerprints on them, Father Michael's. However, in the indecent picture there was a small image of another adult's reflection in a mirror. The lab technicians were able to enhance the image and it revealed another priest taking part in the lewd act as well. It wasn't Father Schmitt though; it was Father Michael's predecessor who died many years before.

Also during the four hours, somehow the media discovered Thomas Michael's double life. Citizens from all over Philadelphia were coming out of the woodwork to curse the late Father Michael's honourable name. There were even other people that cried they too were molested by Father Michael. Furthermore, once the media found out about Father Michael's unlawful behaviour, someone leaked the information about Mark Keller and Wanda Slone's past conduct.

By 8 P.M., Captain Baron returned from his meeting with the chief of police and the mayor of the city. Upon his entrance into the precinct, the captain called all the detectives working on capturing Kevin Mason into his office. As soon as the detectives entered his office, they could tell by his demeanour that he wasn't a happy person. "You don't look too good,

Captain," Detective Ronald stated, as he sat in a chair across from the captain's desk.

"Well, you try having your ass chewed out by the mayor for over two hours and see how that makes you feel," Captain Baron shouted angrily. "The mayor is on the verge of a heart attack because he feels we can't do our jobs. Ever since the news found out that the man we believe is behind the murders has killed only indecent unsuspected criminals, a vast number of people of this city have started to support him. They're now calling our suspect the Vigilante Killer. The mayor is afraid that this might start a following where people feel they can take the law into their own hands and get away with it because we can't get our act together, and always seem to be two steps behind!

"Kevin Mason is becoming a royal pain in my ass, and I want this scumbag off the streets before he kills again. Now I'm not saying that I'm upset that three disgraceful dirtbags were murdered because God knows how many more victims they would have harmed if they'd gone on living. But I'm saying it wasn't up to Mason to kill them. The last time I checked, he has to follow the law like everyone else."

When Captain Baron's lips stopped moving, Detective Seff stood up and calmly responded, "I don't know what else we can do to capture Mason. We've followed every lead we have. We have patrol units staked out twenty-four hours a day, at every location there is a high probability he'll show up. We even have his face printed on the cover of almost every newspaper in the Philadelphia area for the past two days. Not to mention on every local news television station."

"Well, we need to do something," Captain Baron declared in a calm, rational voice. "Because if we don't come up with something in the next twenty-four hours, the mayor's calling in the Feds and we're officially off the case." The last thing the detectives or the captain wanted was to lose the investigation to someone else. It only shows failure and unreliability, especially if the subsequent law enforcement agents solve the case or capture a suspect they couldn't.

As luck would have it, two hours later, a man called claiming he knew the whereabouts of Kevin Mason. "Nine-one-one, is this an emergency?"

"The man, the man in the paper, the one they say killed all those people, Kevin Mason, I saw him."

"Okay, sir, and where did you see him?" the police operator asked.

"I only touched him once, you have to believe me. I was just looking for a place to sleep and there he was face down," the mysterious man answered, breathing heavily, avoiding the operator's question.

"Sir, please try and calm down. I assure you if you did nothing wrong, there isn't anything to worry about. Just tell me where you believe you saw Kevin Mason."

"I think I saw him under the West End Bridge on the south side," the man finally answered.

"And what is your name, sir?" the operator asked next. However, the strange man answered by hanging up the phone. The phone operator wasn't able to pinpoint the location from where the call was made because it came from a prepaid disposable phone, and the individual didn't stay on the line long enough. After the phone call was terminated, the operator followed protocol and telephoned Detective Garder. Terry informed Detective Seff immediately of the location, and all of the detectives, including the captain, left the precinct swiftly. They took three different squad cars and sped toward the West End Bridge one behind the other.

The West End Bridge crosses over the Ohio River. The foundation of the bridge is located underneath the bridge, but rests above a lowland region saturated with water, which bears a slight resemblance to a swamp. The region is typically deserted because it's unfit for habitation or use. However, the area is sometimes a temporary home to an occasional floater, drifting from place to place. It is also an excellent place to hide oneself.

Detective Seff and the others raced down Route 65 and exited onto Reedsdale Street. Reedsdale Street ran perpendicular under the West End Bridge and was the closest road to the foundation. When the officers reached the bridge, they jumped out of their cars with their pistols in one hand, and their flashlights in the other. From a short distance, it looked like little rays of light floating in the air, charging toward the desolate area.

The land area under the bridge wasn't large so there weren't many places to hide. However, it was night and the region wasn't lit at all. The officers were depending on the moonlight and their flashlights to lead the way. The officers decided to spread out, but to stay close in order to communicate, just in case danger arose. As the officers walked closer to the foundation, they found themselves walking around numerous thin barked trees, and through soft wet mud, marsh, and small streams of filthy water. Not the type of terrain to be walking around in wool suits and leather shoes.

As the officers rummaged through the squalid territory, Detective Russ noticed an object in the distance shaped like a body. After he quietly communicated his finding to the other officers, they all started to move toward the object, pointing their weapons and flashlights in its general direction. When the officers stood at a short distance from the object, it became apparent that it was a human body. At that point, the captain commanded the officers to halt and find cover behind the bark of a tree.

"Kevin Mason," Captain Baron shouted. "This is the Pittsburgh police department. You're wanted for questioning of the deaths of Father Michael, Mark Keller, and Wanda Slone. Now we just want to talk, so there is no reason to be hostile in any way."

The captain's statements went unanswered and the body still didn't move. None of the officers was sure if the person was asleep, playing dead, or actually deceased, so the captain instructed the detectives to move closer with precaution. The closer they came to the object it became obvious that the body was without life, floating face down in a bayou.

Chapter 24

The body belonged to Kevin Mason, and he was shot once in the right temple. His eyelids managed to stay open, but his eyes weren't visible because they rolled to the back of his head. A nine millimetre silver gun was found by the edge of the bayou. The clip was empty and so was the chamber of the gun. Mason's dead body reeked of a disturbing odour, along with the rest of the dark clothes. His skin swelled and became awfully wrinkly, which is normal when a body has been soaking in water for a period of time.

Crime scene specialists were on the scene within an hour. They set up high powered lights all around the area where Kevin's body was found. This made it easier for everyone to see and examine the area for evidence. There were two theories floating around on how Kevin came to pass. The first and popular view was suicide; the other less believable theory was murder. "If you ask me, the poor bastard just couldn't take the voices in his head anymore. Came out here, pointed the gun at his head, shot himself, dropped the gun on the ground, and fell over into an oversized puddle," Detective Ronald commented.

"There's nothing in his pockets except an empty prescription bottle," Detective Russ stated, as he picked himself up from searching the dead body. The label on the bottle read Risperidone, which is an atypical antipsychotic medication. Risperidone is often used to treat delusional psychosis, including schizophrenia. "I've actually read somewhere that people who suffer from schizophrenia have a higher rate of suicide than the general population. It's very possible that the voices in his head drove him to commit suicide."

"Well, if you look at his skin around the entry wound, there are signs of charring," Detective Seff stated, as he bent down toward Mason's head to take a closer look. "When a bullet enters the human body shot at close range, and I'm only talking in terms of two to three inches, hot gases emanate from the gun and burn the skin, just like it did with our corpse here. Two or three inches places the gun in the perfect range for suicide. And I'm almost certain that the medical examiner will find bullet fragments embedded in his skin near the wound, which is also caused by close range shooting. What do you think, Captain?"

"The pieces of the puzzle seem to fit perfectly," Captain Baron replied. "A schizo running around killing people because the voices in his head tell him to, doesn't take his meds, points the gun at himself and takes his own life. Not particularly the ending I had in mind, but either way our number one suspect is dead and this case is closed.

"Listen, I know it's late, and you've all been working since early this morning, but there's still work to be done. I need you all to look around this area and try to find any evidence that might pertain to this shooting. Remember, every little bit helps. When you feel that you have completed a diligent search, call it a night, come back here again tomorrow during light hours, and comb the area again. I'm going to take the gun to ballistics and have a fingerprint analysis done. I'm also going to instruct the medical examiner to have an autopsy report on my desk by first thing tomorrow morning. That way we'll know more about the body. Any questions?" the captain asked, but didn't allow time for the detectives to respond. "Good, that's all for now."

The detectives stayed for a couple of hours before they decided to call it a night. They didn't find very much evidence, except for a couple of boxes of food that they bagged for fingerprints. Kevin Mason's body was transported to the medical examiner's office an hour before the detectives decided to come back tomorrow morning. However, the detectives never made it back to the swampy area. They each received a phone call around 4:30 in the morning from Captain Baron to report to the station at 6:30 A.M. instead.

A half an hour before the captain telephoned the detectives, he received a phone call from Dr. Sachs precisely after he performed the autopsy on Kevin Mason. The good doctor informed the captain that there wasn't any evidence that disproves the act of suicide, but he was positive that the body had been dead for at least three days. That made it impossible for Mason to have murdered any of the victims. "It's true, the cold water in which Kevin Mason's body was found might have delayed the normal changes of body decomposition," Dr. Sachs explained. "But I found small amounts of blowfly larvae in his hair, and our analysis of the larvae compared with the most recent decomposition studies suggests that Mason has been deceased for at least seventy-two hours."

By six thirty, all the detectives were in Captain Baron's office drinking a cup of coffee for the rush of caffeine. "I hope everyone had a nice rest because we have a lot of work to do today," the captain articulated. "Did anyone by any chance catch the morning news? Because the press is having a field day knowing that the police's number one suspect was dead before the murders even began. I don't know how they discovered this information so quickly, but I bet the real killer is laughing his ass off. And you know what, he should be, because he's killed three people and we've been looking for a dead suspect this whole time.

"This is our last day to find that son of a bitch. However, I can almost guarantee the chief will call me sometime this morning, informing me that we are no longer in charge of this investigation. The humiliation we caused this department alone gives him enough reason." The captain paused briefly and sat quietly for a moment shaking his head left to right.

"A crime scene specialist found a bullet wedged in the bark of a tree earlier this morning," the captain continued. "It says in the ballistic report that the bullet has traces of Kevin Mason's blood and tissue on it. However, I don't know if Mason's death was a suicide, or if someone else pulled the trigger. I don't even know if there's a connection between his death and the other murders. Ergo, I don't know if the bullet would even help this investigation!"

"You know last night while I was sifting through piles of mud," Detective Seff interjected. "Something was bothering me in the back of my mind, but I couldn't put my finger on it. Then when I woke up this morning it occurred to me. When the individual broke into my apartment and hit me over the head with a gun, he was holding it in his left hand. Kevin Mason was shot in the right temple. If I was going to use a gun to commit suicide, I would have used my good, stronger hand."

"Yeah, but even if Mason didn't kill himself, and he was in fact murdered, there still isn't any evidence linking his death to the other three victims," Russ retorted.

"Think about it," Seff replied. "If the person behind the killings knew of Kevin Mason, his past, and the fact that we'd go looking for him, believing it was him behind the murders, the real killer knew it would give him plenty of time to murder, plan, and kill again without any fear of being caught."

"So you're saying whoever's behind these murders purposely killed Mason, dumped his body at a location where no one would find him, or care to report it, and then went on a killing spree, using Mason's MO? All so we would be distracted pooling our resources together to locate Kevin Mason," Ronald pondered.

"Exactly right, he mind fucked us," Detective Seff responded.

"If that's true then we walked right into his little scheme, didn't we," the captain stated. "All right, since this is the best and only lead we have right now, I need all of you to start cross-referencing Kevin Mason's family, friends, co-workers, doctors or anyone else you can think of that might know vital information about Mason's criminal past. See if any red flags pop up, and remember time is our enemy, so work as quickly and diligently as possible. That's all for now, you're dismissed."

The detectives quickly went back to their desks and grabbed all the files and reports pertaining to the murders. Then they took the documents and moved them into the first open conference room they could find, so they could work together. As Seff was going through Father Michael's file, he came across something that he didn't notice before. He quickly picked himself up from his chair, and excused himself from the room.

Detective Seff didn't return to the conference room until an hour later. Upon his return, he told the other detectives to grab their jackets because he believed he knew exactly who was behind the killings. They quickly grabbed their jackets and left the precinct with him.

Chapter 25

"This is Tom Shoel with a Channel Twelve news report. I am standing outside in front of Zone One Pittsburgh police station where we have just learned that sometime earlier this morning police investigators escorted a possible suspect in the Vigilante Killings inside the precinct. The police have not publicised the name of the suspect as of yet, but they did promise to keep the people of Pittsburgh updated on any breaking news. After speaking with several local residents in the area, I received mixed reactions to the capture of the possible killer. Some of the residents felt safer walking the streets knowing someone is protecting them from criminals, and others felt the killer's actions is nothing short of an act of lunacy. If any other news breaks in the investigation, you can be sure you'll hear it here first, on Channel Twelve News. I'm Tom Shoel, back to you, John."

Inside the police station, Detective Seff was prepping to interrogate Irving Adelson, the former detective who originally captured Kevin Mason over thirty years ago. Irving was being held in a small interrogation room without any windows, alone for over three hours. Furthermore, he was handcuffed to a bar connected to a table fastened to the floor. The room had no mirrors or hidden tape recorders.

It did however, have a small video feed where others could watch in on an upstairs monitor. Seff thought it would be best to grill the suspect alone, so Irving wouldn't feel crowded and uncomfortable. But it was Captain Baron's decision that allowed the detective to question Irving privately. "I only want you talking about what we can prove. Leave the bullshit out of the room," the captain instructed. "I want him to know we have him by the balls. And remember, Irving has been read his rights, therefore, if he decides to lawyer up, your questioning ceases immediately. I don't want this bastard walking free on some procedural informality. Now, I'll be watching upstairs along with Detectives Ronald and Russ, so if you need anything, just walk out of the room and I'll come and meet you down here. Give me ten seconds to run upstairs, and then enter the interrogation room. Good luck."

Holding a rather thick expanded file under his right arm, Detective Seff entered the room and sat down across from Irving. As soon as their eyes met, Irving gave the detective a cold wicked look and said nothing. Seff on the other hand stared with a gloating grin. "I've been told you've been read your rights, and if at anytime you decide that this conversation should end, your decision will be complied with," the detective stated.

"Listen, I know the law, I know my rights, and I know them well. I've sat in your seat before; I've done your job. I know your little interrogation tactics probably better than you do. I also know I'm innocent, and you can't possibly have anything on me. So, I'll be leaving here in forty-eight hours," Irving replied.

"No offence to you, sir, but you worked one case that you successfully fumbled, and then you rode a desk for the remainder of your career. You know nothing about what it's like to be a real detective," Seff retorted. "And the law is a wonderful thing, until people decide to defy it and believe they can act above it. That's why I bust my ass building cases against these people, and I do my best to put them away for a very long time. And as you can see by the size of this file in front of me, I've built a pretty solid case against you. So, you should start learning to get comfortable in tight quarters such as this room, because you'll be staying in one a lot longer than forty-eight hours," the detective said, staring Irving dead in the eyes with determination.

Irving sat back in his chair, as far back as the manacles would allow him to move. "You're bluffing, Detective," Irving replied. "But I am interested in what you think you have on me."

Detective Seff opened the cover of the expanded file, but stopped there. "Do you remember that day when my partner and I showed up at your apartment, I mentioned the name Father Thomas Michael to you? You said the name sounded familiar but you didn't know who he was?"

"Yeah, I vaguely remember saying something like that, so what?"

"Did you know that Thomas Michael wasn't just a preacher, he was also a photographer? He even liked to be in some of the pictures himself. But don't take my word for it; take a look for yourself," the detective said, as he reached into the file and took out ten pre-selected photographs. He laid them down in front of Irving to view. "We found the pictures hidden inside a wall safe in the priest's private office.

"When I first looked at the photographs, I didn't recognise any of the youngsters. Yet, at the same time, I could sense a familiarity with one of the children. It was as if I've seen an image of that child before, but I couldn't place my finger on where I've seen the kid. Then it dawned on me, I saw a picture of the very same child in your apartment that day I visited. Do you recognise the boy I'm referring to, Mr. Adelson?" the detective asked.

Irving stayed quiet and just stared at the pictures one by one while Seff waited for an answer. However, minutes of silence convinced the detective to relinquish a response to his own question. "I'm almost positive you could identify one of the children in the photographs. I only say this because after we arrested you, we searched through your apartment and we found several pictures of the same child. Therefore, I'm already aware that you know exactly who this child is." Still intently looking at the pictures, Irving started to grind his teeth, and held his breath for moments at a time, but continued to sit silently. "We also discovered other interesting related pictures in your apartment; pictures of this boy growing up into a young adult, and eventually an older man. He grew up to look exactly like you."

Detective Seff felt that Irving wanted to say something, but still decided to sit quietly and not utter a response. "Let me ask you something," the detective posed. "How many times did Thomas Michael touch you in places that still haunt you today? How many times did he make you participate in sexual acts you never wanted to perform?" As each question flowed from the detective's mouth, the tone of his voice grew louder. "How embarrassed and humiliated did he make you feel that you never spoke a word about what he did to you to anyone? You kept it bottled up inside, like a ticking time bomb. But you had your revenge, didn't you, when you visited the priest last Wednesday night at St Paul's Church? You shot him three times, payback for what he did to you!"

"I did no such thing," Irving answered, outraged at the accusation. "I haven't been to that church since I was six years old. I don't even have any recollection of even being alone in the same room with Father Michael. And what do these pictures prove other than the late Father Michael was a sick man. You know detective, this isn't like the old days where you can just pin a murder on someone without proof," Mr. Adelson stated as he brought his voice to a calm.

"Keep your pants on; I'm not finished just yet. Your next victim, Mark Keller, was an old neighbourhood friend of yours from back in the day. I'm sure you remember him, the two of you played on the same high school baseball team together. He was even a guest at your wedding. I was able to contact your ex-wife earlier today. She wasn't an easy person to find, but I finally tracked her down in London.

"She told me that you and Mr. Keller were best friends since you were little. She also said you had a bond like brothers, which would explain why you did nothing to stop his extracurricular activities of murdering deaf-mute women."

"If you're expecting a rise out of me from your mere accusations, you're not going to get one," Irving told the detective.

The detective briefly paused, moved the extended file to the side, and sat back in his chair. "Mr. Adelson do you know why your ex-wife divorced you?"

Irving gave Detective Seff a cold, dead stare and replied, "Irreconcilable differences."

"Do you mind elaborating?"

"As a matter of fact I do." Irving responded. "I don't see what that has to do with anything."

"Motive," the detective answered.

"I don't know what you're talking about."

"Your ex-wife told us that it was her who wanted a divorce, because she was having an affair, and after ten years together she wasn't in love with you anymore. She claims she never told you whom she was having an affair with. However, she said you called her not too long ago, very drunk and very upset. Crying and screaming about how she slept around with your best friend, Mark Keller.

"All this time you protected his secret, while he had an affair with your wife at the time. It must have driven you insane when he recently told you?"

"I didn't murder Mark," Irving interrupted, "and as for my ex-wife, we divorced some time ago, and I learned to live with it and moved on with my life."

"Moved onto booze and hookers you mean?" Detective Seff declared.

"I don't know what you're talking about," Irving answered promptly. "Booze maybe, but hookers, I don't think so."

"It became a routine for you. After work you found yourself a bottle, sometimes two, got drunk, and went searching for company." Irving snickered at the preposterous notion, but the detective kept pushing the idea. "God knows how many prostitutes you had the pleasure of frolicking with. It must have cost you a pretty penny though. Yet, there was one girl who sometimes didn't charge you for the price of admission. A girl you fell in love with who in turn fell in love with you.

"You made her feel comfortable from the harsh world she was forced to live in. Her name was Wanda Slone," the detective uttered, as he pulled out a picture from Wanda's crime scene photos to show Mr. Adelson.

Irving studied the picture for a moment, and then told the detective, "I'm sorry, I don't know who the woman in this picture is, and I never heard the name Wanda Slone before."

"Really," the detective replied surprisingly. "Well, maybe you've heard of the name Tahleek Jackson?"

"Nope, I've never heard that name either," Irving answered confidently.

"I'm surprised to hear that because Mr. Jackson feels he knows you very well, and claims you knew Wanda Slone even better. He told us a little story about how he introduced the two of you, well, after you paid him in advance." Detective Seff started to notice a slight change in Irving's pleasant demeanour and believed if he kept pressing the facts explained to him by Tahleek; Irving might make some guilty admittance out of anger. "Tahleek also said you became one of the best repeat customers, and that he can also provide other witnesses who could corroborate everything he told me."

"If you want to believe the word of a low-life pimp and his friends, well you go right ahead," Irving interjected, taking offence to the very notion of him having to pay for sexual relations. "But I don't know any Tahleek Jackson, and I never touched a hooker in my life!"

"In any case, Tahleek said that your relationship with Wanda grew into something more than just business. He said it was some type of adoration for each other. That sometimes you would spend days with her alone and she would forget to show up to work, which in turn caused a problem for Tahleek. The more time Wanda spent with you, the less time she was out producing money for her pimp.

"Unexpectedly, Tahleek paid you a visit and clearly explained the consequences of your bond with Wanda. Then all of a sudden, you ended your relationship with her and she cursed the day she ever met you. Tahleek must have been pretty convincing since you're a police officer, and he should be the one afraid of you. What was it he had over your head that he was willing to bury you with, or was it that he threatened to hurt Wanda?"

Irving didn't respond at first, and took a moment to collect his thoughts. "I know what you're trying to do and it's not going to work," he said calmly. "The bottom line is you can't prove I ever had any relations with Wanda Slone; except for the word of a thug who probably has a long rap sheet. Not to mention, even if I knew Wanda and cared about her as you say I did, then why would I kill her? Huh? Answer me that."

"Well, soon after your relationship with Wanda ended, she found out she was pregnant." Suddenly, Irving's face presented a puzzled look, but it swiftly vanished. "She decided to keep the baby, and not get an abortion. Wanda went through nine hard months of pregnancy and then for some unknown reason, murdered her own child minutes after it was born. Ironically, the child's deceased body was found in a dumpster and murdered the same way his mother was found.

"I know what you're probably thinking; Wanda was a hooker and most likely slept with many men. Therefore, the child could belong to any one of them. However, Tahleek mentioned Wanda found out she was pregnant soon after your relationship with her ended. And if I had to guess how many men Wanda had unprotected sex with, or at least acted more lax with the very concept, you would be the only man I could think of.

"My guess is that you found out about Wanda's pregnancy and the fact that she killed your child, which is exactly why you murdered her. Payback for what she did to your newborn child."

The detective's allegations left a smirk on Irving's face. "Detective, you're telling lies again. I don't know how many ways I can explain this to you, but I don't know any Wanda Slone."

"Mr. Adelson, after we arrested you, we searched your apartment. During that search, we found samples of your hair stuck to a comb you keep in your bathroom. We found enough hair to gather a DNA sample and use it for a standard paternity test. After comparing the DNA of both Wanda's deceased child, and your own, it came back a positive match. So why don't you cut the shit and stop lying."

Irving slammed his fists against the table in rage. "So I knew Wanda Slone, but I didn't know she was pregnant, or that it was my child. And I certainly didn't know she killed it!" he continued to yell. "Now I've been sitting here listening to you make accusations of murder, but nothing you have said or shown me proves I killed anyone. Sure, you think you've discovered motive, but you need physical evidence that actually ties me to the murders, which you don't have, and will never get. Which is why you're trying to scare me into admitting I was behind these killings, but like I told you before, I know your tricks and they aren't going to work on me. So just do me a favour; stop wasting my time with your phony allegations."

Right after Irving's temper tantrum, Detective Seff reached into his expanding file and pulled out a plastic bag labelled evidence. The detective then placed the bag on the table in front of Mr. Adelson. "Inside the bag are the bullets that killed all three of the victims. Forensic specialists examined each bullet and found small amounts of each victim's blood and tissue. They also discovered that it came from the same gun Kevin Mason supposedly used to kill himself with. So, maybe you can explain how these bullets wound up in a small lockbox, hidden under a loose wooden panel in the closet of your apartment. Can you answer me that?"

Irving quickly denied the assertion. "There is no way those bullets were in my apartment unless someone put it there," he shouted. "I mean, yes, I own a lockbox which I keep a gun in for extra security, but I never stored those bullets in it."

"Well, we never discovered any gun, just the bullets."

"Is this another one of your mind games again, Detective?"

"I'm afraid not. Father Michael wasn't the first person you murdered, was it? My guess is, by some chance, you ran into Kevin Mason, and you immediately recognised the face of the man who ruined your career, and killed those people years ago. You couldn't help but follow him around, and over time you learned where he lived, where he worked, and his normal weekly routine. At first maybe you were only planning to kill him, but when you saw him walk into Father Michael's church, you started thinking about an even bigger plan, a killing spree of all the people that wronged you. And why not, you had the perfect fall guy. A person you knew had a history of a severe mental deficiency, and has previously murdered before. Someone you knew the police would immediately suspect as the killer.

"So you murdered Mason first, making it look like he committed suicide. Then you dumped the body in an oversized puddle near the foundation of the West End Bridge. A spot that would slow his body decomposition and a place you knew the chances of him being found were unlikely. And once Mason was out of the way, you were able to start killing the others, starting with Father Michael.

"At first we started chasing a suspect who committed murders with the same MO that suddenly disappeared without his meds, coincidentally at the same time the killings began. We became positive it just couldn't be coincidence, while all the time you're killing the victims and we're chasing a corpse. You killed each victim one after the other in small increments of time, so it would appear their deaths came after his. Then after you killed Wanda Slone, you returned to where you murdered Kevin Mason and neatly placed the gun close to his body. Soon after planting the gun, you made an anonymous phone call to the police where they could find Mason, so we could hold him responsible for all the murders!"

"I'm telling you, I had nothing to do with the murders of those people." Irving yelled with frustration.

"I have to give you credit though, because your plan almost worked. However, the cold water you threw Kevin Mason in, to throw off his time of death, housed insect larvae. And the medical examiners found small amounts of it in Mason's hair, making it possible to approximate his time of death before the others."

Irving sat quietly thinking, shaking his head back and forth. "No, there's no way. Someone's doing this to me. I'm being framed; you have to believe me. I'm being framed, goddamn it!" Irving yelled, raising himself from his seat. "I had nothing to do with those murders. Get these handcuffs off of me!" he shouted, trying to pull the handcuffs free from the table.

Just moments after Irving started becoming defiant, Detective Russ and Ronald came barging into the interrogation room and restrained Irving. They quickly escorted him into a holding cell, where he could calm down in solitude. As Irving was being taken away, the captain walked over to Detective Seff and asked, "Why do you think he kept the bullets?"

"If I had to guess, I'd say he kept them as trophies," the detective answered. "I'd like to talk to him some more in a little while when he calms down. I still have some more questions to ask him."

"I don't think that's a good idea. You saw how hardheaded the man was. I don't think he's going to admit to anything, and we have enough evidence to put him away anyway. He'll lawyer up and come to his senses. Then he'll try and make a deal just like every other criminal, only he'll be lucky if the district attorney offers him a life sentence with the possibility of parole."

Chapter 26

The very next morning, the captain called Seff into his office and introduced him to his new partner, Christine Santamaria. Christine was a new detective but like most other detectives, not new to the police force. She has been a law enforcement agent for six years, and was recently promoted to detective status. Before the promotion, Christine worked deep undercover in an underground drug smuggling operation. That was until her cover became compromised and she had to be pulled out of the field for fear of her life.

After the captain introduced the two detectives, he assigned them to investigate a robbery that ended in felony murder. "Just listen to everything Detective Seff tells you to do and you'll be just fine. He's our best detective." The captain informed her and then dismissed them both.

Before they left for the crime scene, Seff quickly grabbed a cup of coffee and purchased a doughnut from the snack machine. He offered to buy a doughnut for Christine, but she denied his kind gesture.

Subsequently they left the station in Detective Seff's car to investigate the homicide case. For the first few minutes of the ride, the detectives didn't say a word to each other, and then Christine decided to break the silence. "As an undercover police officer, I worked alone, so you'll have to give me time to adjust to this situation. I'm told I usually talk too much. So if I seem distant and quiet, it's only because I'm just not used to the idea of having a partner yet."

"That's okay," Detective Seff assured Christine. "I guess it's normal to be a little shy when you first meet someone. I'm just hoping you won't turn out to be a homicidal killer like my last partner," Seff chuckled to himself.

"I just read something about that in this morning's newspaper. It said you two were partners for quite a while."

"Eight years to be exact. I'm just sorry he decided to throw his entire life away. But we can't dwell on the past," Detective Seff insisted. "So, tell me about yourself."

"Well, there isn't really much to tell," Christine replied. "I grew up in Long Beach, New York, raised only by my mother. I came down to Pennsylvania to attend college, and during that time, my mother became deathly ill and passed away. Since I had no reason to go back to New York, I decided to stay in Pennsylvania. I became a police officer straight out of school, worked undercover for the past four years, and now I'm working as a homicide detective. What about you? What's your story?"

"I grew up around these parts of Pittsburgh. My family moved from place to place a lot, but mostly only around the same area. Growing up, I saw this neighbourhood change from good to worse, and ever since I was little, I had this dream of cleaning it up. I guess law enforcement was just in my blood. I was always the kid who broke up a fight, or stuck up for someone who couldn't fight for themselves. So after college, like you, I joined the police force.

"So we have some things in common," Christine noted. "I've also noticed some other things we have in common."

"Oh yeah, what's that?" the detective inquired.

"Well, we both drive with two feet, we're right handed, we both take three packs of sugar with our coffee, and we both have scars on the top of our heads, but on different sides," Christine replied. "Only your scar looks like it might have hurt a little more than mine," she uttered while flipping her hair to the side, so she could show Seff her thin lined scar. "I had it ever since I was a nine years old. My mother gave me a Pogo Stick for my birthday that year. I was getting good at it, until I cracked my head open when I fell into the side mirror of our neighbour's car. It took six stitches to close the gash. What about you, how did you get yours?"

"It's a long story of a childhood memory I don't care to remember."

Chapter 27

The Revealing

I have killed people from all walks of life. I never cared how bad their lives have been, or how good they had it. Just their ability to commit crimes so immoral, it makes even the devil blush. I only murder those who deserve to die, and should be punished for what they have done. For me, it isn't only about whom they've killed, stabbed, raped, poisoned, or molested. It's also about their sadistic capabilities they are able to carry out and come to terms with.

Irving Adelson wasn't the first person who took responsibility for murders I have brutally committed. But like all my prey, it was well deserved. Irving really did murder Kevin Mason, and then tried to cover it up by making it look like a suicide. He would have got away with it too, if I never decided to alter fate. However, that's why I was put here: to change the power that predetermines events.

I didn't meet Irving for the first time that day I went to see him with my ex-partner at his apartment. I met him two days prior, the day after he executed Kevin Mason. It was just luck that I met Irving though. I saw him at a bar sharing a drink with some of his old work buddies from the force. The bar is a common place for off-duty cops to kick back and relax after a hard day of work. I was at the bar sharing a drink with Mitchell.

I noticed Irving seconds before he sat down with his friends. You could say he stood out amongst the rest of the crowd. His aura was anything but pure. I didn't approach Irving until after he left the bar. I followed him outside, excusing myself to smoke a cigarette. As he was saying goodbye to his friends, I lightly brushed my hand against his arm. Unbeknownst to Irving, I knew everything about him and everything about the people in his life before he even reached his car.

The images I saw, not only coming from Irving, but from my last three victims as well, were atrocious acts against morality so devious that it called for punishment. That's why they're no longer walking side by side with the living. It wasn't hard to create a strategic plan of three murders and have Irving take the fall, for I had all the information I ever needed in my head. Typically, Irving would be lying six feet under with the rest of my victims, only I had a slight dilemma. Father Michael was a prominent figure in the eyes of the public, and his murder wouldn't have gone unnoticed.

When you kill a well-known person like the illustrious Father Michael, the media gets involved and people take notice, which creates pressure upon certain people to act. For instance, the public compels the mayor to take action; then the mayor insists that the chief of police run a more sufficient workforce, and eventually, the pressure lingers down to the rest of the police personnel to do whatever it takes to get the job done. Moreover, the force behind the pressure increases as time goes on. It doesn't just go away dropped in a pile of unsolved mysteries. That's why Irving Adelson had to live, so he could take responsibility for my decision to kill.

The way Irving lived his life made him an easy target. The man lived like a hermit and stayed in his apartment almost twenty-four hours a day by himself. As a result of his lifestyle, there isn't a person to corroborate his alibi of being home when the murders took place. Finding the gun Irving used to kill Kevin Mason was easy; it was placed next to his cold body where he was murdered. I originally found Mason's corpse lying on stable ground already infested with all sorts of insects. Therefore, in order for my plan to be more believable, I dumped Mason in a pool of wintry water to make it appear as if someone was trying to slow down Mason's body decomposition.

I killed each victim one by one, and made it look like Kevin Mason was the one behind each murder, knowing the whole time it would be Mr. Adelson who would ultimately suffer the consequences. I murdered Father Michael and Mark Keller the same night one after the other. I didn't kill Wanda until the following evening, although I did meet her before I murdered Mr. Keller. I approached her in a disguise, and made her an offer she couldn't decline.

I fabricated the sexual encounter with Wanda, the masked man in my bedroom, and the way he hit me on the back of the head with his gun. It was actually me who inflicted the wound upon my head, though I injured myself more than I expected to. Nevertheless, I wasn't really in a lot of pain. I acted more hurt than I may have led others to believe. But all the same, it looked believable.

Mitchell Jacobs' intrusive copycat act wasn't a huge interference to my scheme. I knew what he did the moment his hand brushed up against mine when he took the cuffs off me from my bedpost that morning. That's how I knew about the bloodstain on the kitchen drawer. Internal affairs would have had a better case against Jacobs if Stephanie, the forensic specialist, didn't overlook the print of Mitchell's ring finger inside the drawer, which he accidentally left behind while sifting through the various knives looking for the sharpest single blade. Luckily, his wife spilled the beans on him.

I placed an anonymous tip to the police where they could find Kevin Mason's body. Then with the help of Father Michael's photographs, I was able to identify Irving as one of the molested, giving him motive for murder and a reason to investigate him further, only to discover he had reason to kill the rest of the victims as well. I had to be sure Irving would be held responsible for each murder, so I planted the bullets in his lockbox during the justifiable search of his apartment.

To tell you the truth, Father Michael never molested Irving Adelson. I stole a half-naked picture of him as a young boy from his ex-wife's apartment. Then I planted it with the other pictures stashed in the priest's wall safe. Irving was telling the truth when he said he never knew he was the father of Wanda Slone's baby, or that she was actually pregnant. But I wonder how he felt knowing the woman he came to love had a child which he probably drove her to murder.

Irving Adelson will live the rest of his life behind bars knowing someone got the better of him. Although he will never know whom that someone is. He'll probably try to appeal whatever guilty verdict he receives hoping the truth will set him free. Yet that won't happen in his lifetime. Instead, he will wither away slowly, day by day, rotting and regretting his horrific decision to take another person's life.

I wouldn't be surprised if people think I am a hypocrite for what I do because in ways I am no different from the people I've come to hunt. Who knows, maybe I am. But if you had the ability to see an individual's iniquities knowing they were willing to do it again and again, and only you had the power to stop them, then what would you do? Would you stand by idly knowing you were sitting next to a child molester lurking for his next victim? Would you be able to overlook the fact that the person eating next to you murdered an innocent mother of two young children? And can you honestly tell me you would be able to ignore a father who abuses his child in ways you can never fathom? Or would you do something about it?